The New Southern Gentleman

Jim Booth

THE NEW SOUTHERN GENTLEMAN

Wexford College Press

MENS SANA INCORPORE SANO

Published as a Wexford College Press paperback 2002
by arrangement with Watchmaker Publishing, Ltd.

ISBN 0-9721786-0-0

Wexford College Press
www.WexfordCollegePress.com
Books@WexfordCollegePress.com

Printed and bound in the United States of America

1 2 3 4 5 6 7 8 9 0

"The Southerner has no mind, merely an attitude…"

Henry Adams

"The days of chivalry are not gone, they are only spiritualized."

Sidney Lanier

I

Daniel Randolph Deal came from two distinguished Virginia families: the Randolphs of Roanoke and the Deals of Lynchburg. The prestige of such ancestors did not enhance his family's business acumen, unfortunately. Chief among the family's financial blunders was his great grandfather's foray into the tobacco business.

After making a fortune in the pulpwood business (recouping the family's losses in the Civil War, or, as *his own* grandfather laughingly called it, the War of Northern Aggression) Great Grandfather Deal looked about for a new venture likely to yield the resounding profits of the pulpwood business. He came across the Brown Company and the Reynolds Company, both in Winston-Salem, North Carolina. Rather than acting prudently and investing moderately in both; the old man followed a hunch and bought hugely in Brown.

Then came the Depression. Great Grandfather Deal died a few years after the Brown Company did.

Grandfather Deal, the current patriarch, continued to operate the pulpwood business into the 1960's, but with increasing ill luck. Finally, he sold most of the remaining timber holdings to a man who sold off the trees, subdivided the land, and made a fortune constructing ranch style homes for the people of Lynchburg and Roanoke. Grandfather Deal then retired to pursue his passion for the history of the South and of his glorious ancestors.

Thus, though the blood of John Randolph of Roanoke flowed in young Daniel Randolph Deal's veins, great wealth, alas, flowed elsewhere.

By American standards, Dan was quite well off; well-to-do might be aptly descriptive. In his own mind, however, Dan was an impoverished aristocrat, one forced to suffer through life with little more than a fine home in a superior neighborhood to live in, excellent clothing to wear, and one of the cheaper Porsches to drive.

Daniel grew up in his grandfather's home. The environment provided by a would-be Southern aristocrat obsessed with family

7

and regional glory might not have been the best for an impressionable sort like Dan Deal. How he got there is a testament of the Southern will.

Dan's father, Augustus Stuart Deal IV, rebelled against the well-modulated inefficiency of his father. He broke with family tradition, attending Virginia Polytechnic Institute and State University instead of the University of Virginia and becoming, instead of the historian his father had hoped, that most practical of types, an engineer.

Stuart, as he was known, further shook the family tree by taking a job with the Department of Highways and working as an on-site coordinator during highway and bridge constructions. It was at one of these sites that he was killed. An I-beam became overbalanced and broke a cable on the crane that was moving it into place. The out of control girder swung into Dan's father, killing him instantly. Dan's grandfather ever after referred to Interstate 81 as: 'The road that killed my eldest son.'

Dan's mother, a career minded interior design major from VPI, albeit with impeccable family credentials from Richmond, was so shocked by her young husband's death that she had a nervous breakdown. Young Dan, then two, was sent to his grandparents until things could be sorted out.

Unfortunately, during her therapy Dan's mother transferred her affection for his father to her psychiatrist, a Frenchman trained in Switzerland visiting the United States as a clinical professor at the Medical College of Virginia. Once she had recovered, she married her therapist, thus making the transference complete.

Grandfather Deal frowned on the union, coming as it did only four years after her husband's death and two years after her recovery. When she came to Lynchburg to reclaim Dan, his grandfather refused to give him up.

"He's a Deal," the old man told her and her dark, slender escort. "A Deal of Virginia. This is where his blood is. This is where he'll remain." His hand tightened on his six-year-old grandson's fingers as the opponents squared off in Grandfather Deal's lawyer's office.

Dan's mother, blonde, with large gray-blue eyes whose features Dan had inherited pleaded quietly, "But he's my son. I need him. I need to see him; to be with him."

"And you shall see him. When you are *here!*" Dan looked up at his grandfather. The old man's voice sounded like God's.

Dan's mother flinched, and the Frenchman patted her arm and spoke to her in a foreign language. She responded in kind. Dan watched them, then turned to his grandfather. The patriarch was looking at the couple in disgust.

Dan's mother recoiled from Grandfather Deal's stare and turned her gaze to her son. He gave her the same scathing look his grandfather had. She gawked pitifully for a moment, then rose from her chair and fled the room. The Frenchman rose, bowed to all present, and followed her. She signed custody of Dan over to his grandfather a few days later.

Thus was Dan's opinion of women and foreigners formed. His grandfather brought him up to be a Southern gentleman. He taught him to be unselfish, moral, and scrupulous. He taught him to be chivalrous to but mystified by women. He taught him to brook no insult. He taught him manners, and he taught him comportment. He tried to make him in his own image.

As he grew up, Dan realized that it was not always easy to follow the strict code of gentlemanliness that his grandfather adhered to. By degrees he came to moderate the precepts he had been taught. Gradually, he reached the conclusion that birth and social position were more important than breeding and behavior in marking out a gentleman.

The reduced circumstances of Dan's family were not so severe as to preclude all private education. He attended Episcopal parochial schools until his high school years. Then, at his own insistence, so as to make himself a more likely candidate for scholarship money, Dan matriculated to public high school.

In high school Dan was editor of his school newspaper, a frequent contributor to the literary magazine (mostly poetry), and, lest he be thought merely an intellectual, co-captain of the tennis team. In fact, he won the state singles title his junior year.

His academic prowess was envied. He eventually graduated third in his class of four hundred. He scored over 1400 on his SAT's and was a National Merit Scholarship semi-finalist. One of his poems was chosen for a national anthology of student poetry. His newspaper won a Columbia University journalism award.

During his senior year, Dan was offered scholarships at both the College of William and Mary and the University of Virginia.

Virginia offered an academic scholarship; William and Mary, a partial academic, partial athletic one. Although flattered by William and Mary's acknowledgement of his athleticism, he opted for the University of Virginia. It was the family school, his grandfather told him. It was the better school, his uncles told him. It was the more prestigious school, Dan decided after reflection. That convinced him.

On the strength of his family's name and his own quiet demeanor, Dan pledged an exclusive fraternity. His uncles paid the difference between his scholarship and his fraternity's dues.

At Virginia Dan again attained some distinction. He was an officer in his fraternity, a student member of the honor council, and a *magna cum laude* graduate, B. A. in English.

Dan decided early in his undergraduate career to attend law school after graduation. Although well suited to the field temperamentally, he decided that becoming an academic was too impractical for one as non-peripatetic as himself. He had written a series of clever, but too obvious poems for the student literary magazine; these convinced him that he was not a writer. There was no family business to enter. He was uninterested in medicine. He had a detached manner and was well spoken. The law seemed the obvious choice.

His excellent undergraduate record and a fine performance on the L.S.A.T. secured scholarship offers from, among others, Wake Forest University in North Carolina. He considered the school with friends who were attending and found it suited him academically and temperamentally. He wished to attend law school somewhere besides Charlottesville. When William and Mary did not offer the level of scholarship support he thought he deserved, the choice was made.

He spent the summer of 1975 leisurely house sitting for one of his English professors in Charlottesville, visiting Lynchburg occasionally to see his family. He read a great deal, all of Austen and most of Dickens. He considered whether he would go to work for his uncle's firm or try for a post with one of the large firms in Richmond. He dreamed of his success and of lovely women.

His future, carefully planned, lay before him, calm and reassuring.

II

Dan Deal first met Alex Radford in late July before they entered law school in September. Wake Forest's housing service had put them in touch with each other. Both were Virginians from similar backgrounds and were entering law students. They seemed well suited.

Wythe Alexander Radford was from Lightfoot, Virginia. A descendant of George Wythe, he had the same impeccable family credentials as Dan. He had attended the College of William and Mary, preferring the social life of that school to the somewhat more academically rigorous curriculum of *the* University of Virginia. He was not, however, of untoward parts academically, having graduated with his B. S. in political science *magna cum laude*.

The last Saturday in July, Dan and Alex met in front of the Wake Forest law library. Alex had spent the previous couple of days visiting a friend from summer camp days who would, coincidentally, also be entering the law school. The friend, one Jason Manetti, had also found a house for Alex and Dan, one right next to his own. All this Alex told Dan as they walked to Dan's car, which sat in a parking lot a few hundred yards away. "Nice car," Alex said as they arrived.

"Thank you." Dan nodded and unlocked the passenger's side door on his Porsche 912. As a high school graduation gift, Grandfather Deal had given Dan the money from an insurance policy of Dan's father's. Dan had used the money to buy the car.

His uncles had felt that perhaps a less expensive car would have left Dan with money for college, but they had acquiesced at their father's insistence that Dan needed the 'right' car, and they have been forced to wince once more at the oft-repeated truth about Dan's 'orphanhood.' Besides, the old man had argued, the money was a gift to the boy from his father.

"My grandfather gave it to me when I graduated from high school." Dan smiled at Alex, then backed out of the parking space and followed Alex's instructions. "Runs well, doesn't it?" Dan downshifted and made a turn. Two sunbathing summer school coeds watched the car admiringly as it passed.

Alex glanced back at them. "I see why you drive this car," he said.

Dan smiled, watching the road. "You're a perceptive man, Alex." He stopped at the intersection leading out of the campus. "Which way?" he asked, glancing at his companion.

"Left."

"Right." Dan started to make a left turn.

"No, left."

Dan pressed the brake and looked at Alex, who smiled mischievously. Dan smiled in return. "Did you say you did your undergraduate work at William and Mary, Alex?" He guided the car down a tree-lined street.

"Yes. They gave me a full scholarship." He shrugged nonchalantly. "And you went to?" Alex asked, in the time honored tradition of lawyers posing a question to which he already knew the answer.

"U.V.A." He glanced at Alex, then back at the road. "Full scholarship." He added with satisfaction, "William and Mary offered me a scholarship, too." He watched Alex out of the corner of his eye to discern his reaction.

"Oh?"

Dan took that as sufficient interest to allow him to continue. "Yes. William and Mary offered me an athletic scholarship."

"What sport?" asked Alex, genuinely surprised, perhaps a bit dubious.

"Tennis. I won the state singles title my junior year in high school." Dan nodded to him knowingly.

Alex snapped his fingers. "Of course. I remember you, Dan. You upset Kennerly. Great match." Alex nodded his own head and looked out at the passing greenery. "Kennerly beat me in the semis the next year," he murmured. Suddenly he gestured. "Turn right, here."

Dan directed the Porsche down a side street. "You played him a great match, Alex." Alex glanced at him and he smiled. "He beat me in the quarters that year," he added wistfully.

"Kennerly's a fine player, isn't he?" Alex said.

"No doubt. He played number one singles at Princeton, you know."

They smiled at each other. Alex pointed down the street. "Pull into that driveway and park beside the white pickup."

Dan did as he was bidden. A short, heavy man, nearly bald, wearing khaki work clothes with a patch over the left breast that read, 'Ernest' came out the front door and down the concrete steps. He grabbed Dan's hand as he and Alex approached the house. "How are y'all boys doing today? My name's Ernest. Ernest Lefever. L-E-F-E-V-E-R. Lefever."

Dan shook hands politely, condescendingly. "I am Daniel Randolph Deal. Of Lynchburg. And this is my friend..."

"Oh, I've met Alex. Met him at Jason's. Next door. Jason Manetti." He pronounced the last name as if he were sounding it out. "He's my tenant, too. Another law student. That's how I met Alex, here." He turned abruptly and led the way into the house.

"My name is Alex. A-L-E-X. Alex," Alex whispered through gritted teeth as Dan motioned him past him. Dan smiled in commiseration.

"Y'all boys will love this house," Lefever said, waving his arms expansively in the small living room. "This here's a quiet street. That street back up there that turns off, Jeffrey Lane, there's some of the younger students there. They get right noisy on the weekends. But here it's quiet. Mostly retired folks; and lawyers like yourselves."

There was a small fireplace in the living room, but that was the best that could be said for it. The kitchen had new linoleum flooring, accented by a tiny refrigerator and tinier stove. The three bedrooms were nondescript enough, one rather smaller than the other two, which Alex suggested could be a mutual study. Lefever followed behind nervously as Dan and Alex examined doors, windows, ceilings, plumbing, and closets throughout the house.

"There's been leakage in the front bedroom closet," Dan said, drawing his head out of the space and turning to Lefever.

"The roof's been completely redone. Just finished about a month ago." Lefever waved his hands at the floor. "Ain't these hardwood floors nice? Refinished them myself."

Alex came in from another bedroom. "Some of the windows need screens. There's no air conditioning, I suppose, and we poor law students can't afford to buy any."

Lefever smiled broadly and played his trump. "There's one of them new heat pumps out back, fellas. Heating and cooling all in one. All hooked up and ready to go."

"The window screens?" Dan said haughtily. Alex glanced his way, surprised at his tone.

Lefever shrugged. "Some of them had holes. They'll be ready next week. I'll have them on the windows before you all are ready to move in." He shifted his weight from one foot to the other. Suddenly he lurched over to the fireplace. "This fireplace is nice, isn't it? It'll be cozy for you and your girlfriends here on winter evenings." He straightened from bending toward the hearth and smiled ingratiatingly, uncertainly.

Alex moved to the front window and watched some children riding bicycles in the street. "Where do we get wood?" he ventured over his shoulder.

Lefever looked apoplectic. Dan came to his rescue. "I can get wood for us, Alex. Are *you* satisfied?" He glanced about disdainfully.

"If you are." Alex shrugged, a perfect mimicry of Lefever's earlier gesture and continued his staring out the window.

Dan, hands in his pockets, turned to Lefever and asked casually, "Well, Mr. Lefever, what is your best rental price?"

Lefever's eyes narrowed and he smiled without opening his mouth. Dan had the impression he was looking at an oversized boiled turnip. "Well, boys," he said slowly, almost condescendingly, "usually I get four hundred for a nice place like this, but seeing as you're *poor law students.*" He looked askance at Alex who made a gesture of helplessness at Dan. "And friends of Jason's, I'll let you have it for three-fifty."

Alex looked at Dan, raised his eyebrows, then shrugged in acquiescence. Dan looked from Alex to Lefever to Alex again. He snorted contemptuously and strode into the kitchen. Out of what he laughingly described once later to friends as class loyalty, Alex followed. As he crossed the room, he glanced at Lefever, frozen at the fireplace. The little man's eyes were unusually wide.

Dan was leaning against the refrigerator, his eyes fixed on the linoleum tiles. He looked up as Alex stopped opposite him. "It's too much, Radford," he said.

Alex shook his head. "I don't think so, Dan. I've checked around the last couple of days. It's a fair price. This is a good place, close to the university. I think we should take it."

They stared at each other for nearly a minute. Then Dan turned abruptly and stalked back into the living room. "Mr. Lefever," he said commandingly, stopping in the center of the room. Lefever looked up from where he knelt by the fireplace, fiddling with the damper. "Alex and I are willing to take this house. Though it is not comparable to our usual standard of living..." He looked out the open front door toward the Porsche; Lefever had done the same, he noted with satisfaction, as he turned back to speak, "We will live here. You must understand, however, that we cannot and indeed, *will not* pay an exorbitant rent. We will pay you three hundred dollars per month. *You* must decide, Mr. Lefever. If you wish *our* sort of people–*gentlemen*–to live here, then you must accept our offer." Dan went to the doorway and looked out across the yard.

Alex, who had come into the room during this exchange, looked on in amazement. Lefever, his mouth open, had risen to his feet, shaking his head slowly from side to side. "Mr.–" he groped, unable to remember Dan's last name.

Dan turned to him and said in a measured tone, "Deal, sir. Daniel Randolph Deal. Of Lynchburg. I thought I had told you." He looked Lefever up and down, calmly, disdainfully.

Lefever started to speak but checked himself. He looked at Alex for explanation, but Alex was looking at Dan in what seemed to Lefever to be an admiring way.

He knew they would be good tenants. He knew, too, that he was being bullied.

"No sir," he said, shaking his head slowly, diffidently, pursing his lips. "I can't afford to do that. Y'all boys would be making me lose money. I've put a lot into this house."

He smiled slyly. Now he'd find out how badly this arrogant college bastard wanted the place.

Alex caught Dan's eye. Dan nodded to him politely and went outside. Alex started to follow, but Lefever cut in front of him and went out after Dan. By the time Lefever had gotten halfway across the yard, Dan had opened the door to his car and was about to get in.

"Mr. Deal," Lefever called, "aren't you willing to discuss this? To negotiate?" He held his hands out in supplication.

Dan regarded him coldly. "There is nothing to discuss, Mr. Lefever. I have explained our position to you. You have rejected it out of hand. There is nothing to negotiate. Good day, sir." He got into the Porsche and closed the door.

As Alex passed Lefever on his way to Dan's car, he paused. "You might want to consider that offer, Mr. Lefever," he said. "You won't get tenants like us very easily. Most first year law students already have places." Alex knew this to be untrue, but he figured it might get the house.

He wanted it. He didn't want to room with Jason Manetti, but he thought it might be interesting to be a short walk from his parties. He'd visited several of Jason's parties during his trips to see friends in Chapel Hill. He'd found them mythic in their decadence.

When he was seated in the car beside Dan, he said, looking straight ahead, "Start the car, Dan. Let it roll back to the street." Dan followed his instructions. As they slowly backed up, Alex waved to Lefever, giving him an exaggerated smile. Lefever waved in return, looking slightly confused, a little regretful. Dan stopped, the car at the street's edge.

Immediately Alex leaped out and called to Lefever. "Excuse me, Mr. Lefever? I didn't catch what you said." He went toward Lefever. Lefever went toward him. They met halfway. After a short conversation, Alex waved Dan back up the driveway.

In the end they signed a one-year lease for three hundred and twenty dollars a month.

As they drove to Elizabeth's Pizza for a late lunch, Dan bemoaned, 'surrendering' the extra rent money. "Oh, Dan," laughed Alex, "surely you won't miss the ten dollars. I'll pay the extra twenty if you like. This will be a good place to live. We might not find another so easily." He thought of the women at Manetti's parties.

"It's not the money, Radford," Dan said, so pointedly that Alex wondered for a moment about his finances. Then he saw the Porsche emblem on the car's dashboard and laughed to himself. Dan continued. "I just don't want someone like Lefever to get the better of me. My family has not always been wise in its business dealings. I intend to do better." Dan pictured to himself the acres of suburbs that had once been Deal timber holdings.

"We did well, Daniel," Alex said calmly. "We were fifty dollars apart. We got thirty back. That's a sixty percent gain for us." He patted Dan's shoulder, then slumped into the bucket seat contentedly. "I think we did the right thing."

They came to a stop sign and Dan turned to him. "We never know, do we Alex?" he asked.

"Know what?"

"If we did the right thing. At least, not until after the fact." Dan pulled into an opening in the traffic.

Alex may have replied, but Dan thought not. Surely he would have heard a response, even above the noise of Steely Dan on the radio and the ring of the Porsche's engine as they sped along. In any event, neither spoke again during the rest of the drive, leading Dan to think that his observation had struck Alex quite forcibly.

III

Dan's new neighbor, Jason Manetti, was not a Virginian. He was not even a Southerner. He hailed from New Jersey, a state known as much for the interstate highways passing through it as for its great universities or its coastal resorts. At least this was true in Dan's South.

Manetti's father was a millionaire plumber. This was true. The father, trained by *his* father in the family trade, was ever mindful of the main chance and turned the modest family business into, 'The largest plumbing and heating contractor in southern New Jersey, also serving eastern Pennsylvania and northern Delaware.'

The father's television commercials, showing him in all his self-confident boorishness, became something of a fad. To his son, of whom many of his classmates at the University of North Carolina would have said those commercials were a glimpse twenty-five years into *his* future, those commercials were a source of acute discomfort. His retaliation to his father's insistence on appearing on television was to spend the old man's money as carelessly as possible. From thence came his reputation at Chapel Hill as a legendary party animal.

Dan and Jason Manetti met briefly when Dan brought Alex Radford back to Manetti's place after lunch. That first meeting was not very cordial; there were too many undercurrents. Dan was formal, officious, stiff. Manetti was casually boorish. A typical North-South confrontation.

"You'll have to excuse Jason's place," Alex said apologetically as they got out of Dan's car, which he'd parked behind Manetti's Corvette in his driveway. Alex led the way up the brick steps onto the flagstone porch.

Dan examined the house. It was old, but in excellent condition, brick with wood frame windows and real working shutters. The front door was shaped like a Roman arch. Alex opened it and called tentatively, "Jason?"

Dan looked past him into a chaotic room. Newspapers lay scattered across the floor; two full ashtrays sat on the arms of an overstuffed chair; a third had overturned and spread its contents across the beige carpet, the gray of cigarette ash punctuated by tan and white cigarette filters, some lipstick stained. A number of empty beer bottles sat on end tables on either side of the sofa.

Jason Manetti appeared through an archway that led to a hallway extending the depth of the house. He was barefoot. He wore no shirt, merely a pair of jeans. He was half a head shorter than either Dan or Alex, although muscular in that way that Dan had always associated with wrestlers in high school.

"Hello, Radford," Manetti said, grinning slyly and glancing, a bit guiltily behind him toward the bedroom door from which he'd emerged. "We… I didn't expect you guys back."

Alex shrugged. "Dealing with Lefever took less time than we thought. Dan, here, got his rent price down thirty dollars." He smiled at Dan, then turned back to Manetti. "Jason, Dan Deal. Dan, Jason Manetti." He smiled graciously, looking first at one, then at the other.

Suddenly, Dan noticed, his smile froze, then disappeared. His face turned scarlet as he looked past Jason down the hallway. Dan's eyes followed his.

They both saw a girl with tousled auburn hair and violet eyes. She had on a man's shirt. Clutched to her chest was a bundle of clothing, probably her own. She looked surprised at them, then guiltily at Alex, then turned and fled down the hall to a room on her left. As she moved away, the tail of her shirt flew up and they saw that she wore no panties.

Once the girl had looked at them, Dan had averted his eyes slightly in a sort of gentlemanly modesty. Alex continued to watch her until she disappeared in a sort of numb amazement.

Finally he asked quietly as the faint sound of a shower began, "Is that…"

"Yeah." Manetti bit off the word. "That's her. She was still here after you had to leave this morning, so *I* invited *her* to stay awhile." He shrugged, then smiled cruelly. "You move, you lose, Radford."

Dan looked from Alex to Jason and back again, comprehending the situation but refusing to believe it true. He looked about the room. "I take it there was a party here last night, Mr. Manetti?" he asked politely.

Manetti looked at him as if he were ineffably stupid. "No shit, Sherlock," he said off-handedly.

Dan calmly reviewed him. "Alex," he said, still looking at Manetti. "I believe Mr. Manetti needs some time to recoup after last night, or...." He held back instead of saying 'this morning,' but said, "So I think I shall visit another time when things are not so... so indisposed." He nodded to them both and turned to go.

Alex followed him to the door. "Dan?"

"Yes?" They faced each other, hidden from Manetti by the half-opened door.

"I'll... my business here is finished. I'm leaving, too. Come help me pack and we'll drive out of town together. I'll show you a short cut out of Winston-Salem." Alex leaned his head toward the bedrooms and raised his eyes in a silent supplication.

Dan stepped past him, back into the room. "Surely, Alex. Glad to help." Alex closed the door gently and they headed back to his bedroom.

Manetti had lit a cigarette and stood leaning against one side of the archway, smoking. He dropped the half-finished cigarette and crushed it on the hardwood flooring of the hallway with his bare foot.

He smiled contemptuously. "Well, if you're leaving, I'm going to get a shower." He ambled slowly down the hallway in front of them, then went into the bathroom where the girl was.

Alex's bedroom was opposite the bathroom. As they quickly packed Alex's things, they could hear first the squeals of the girl as Manetti joined her in the shower, then a sound like someone slapping a tile wall. As they emerged from the bedroom with Alex's suitcase, the girl's squeals had become moans, interspersed by grunts from Manetti.

Dan shook his head and made his way toward the front door. He turned when he realized that Alex wasn't following.

Alex stood silent in the hallway, his face stony, his knuckles white as he gripped the suitcase handle.

"Leave it, Alex," Dan said gently. Alex looked at him, then at the bathroom door again. He smiled forcedly, shrugged his shoulders, and followed Dan outside.

After he had tossed his belongings into his car, Alex leaned against it and looked across at the house he and Dan had just rented. "You know," he said, tapping the car's roof, "she's really not like that. Last night we talked about all kinds of things: poetry, religion, philosophy. I read Keats to her." He sighed. "Damned women. They win every time."

Dan leaned against the car beside him. "You were up against completely unscrupulous forces, Alex. A Yankee and a woman. Either will do anything to obtain its desired ends." Alex looked at him askance, unsure he could believe his ears. The perfectly serious look on Dan's face assured him he could.

Alex burst into laughter. "You're all right, Dan Deal." He looked over his shoulder at Manetti's house. "To hell with them," he said. "Follow me. I'll lead you out of town. I'll call in a few days to arrange our moving in."

Dan stepped back to allow Alex to open his car door. Alex motioned him down to the car window after he'd gotten in. "Thanks for helping me keep my sense of humor about that." He glanced toward Manetti's.

Dan smiled and saluted cavalierly, then walked over to his own car. He stood beside it looking at Manetti's place, trying to picture the girl again. Usually he could remember people's faces well after only a glance, but for some reason he couldn't recall hers clearly at all.

Alex, already in the street, blew his horn. Dan waved to him and got into his car. He looked at the house one last time. All he could picture was soft, disheveled auburn hair and what looked like violet eyes. He thought of Alex's pained face upon finding her faithless. His opinion of women was reconfirmed.

He followed Alex out of Winston-Salem. He did not think of the girl again. Instead, he puzzled over Alex's laughing response to his comment about Yankees and women.

IV

Moving was done; they were settled. Dan had asked for and received the largest bedroom. In return, he used part of his room as his study, leaving the tiny third bedroom for Alex's use, an arrangement that pleased both. Alex openly because he was happy to have so much space and such a generous roommate, Dan secretly because the arrangement gave him his privacy and satisfied his need for a certain amount of selfish cloistering.

Both Alex and Dan were serious students. They found first-year law school a consuming experience and spent nearly as much time in the law library as at home. Their mealtimes, social lives, relationship; all came to revolve around their studies.

They found Jason Manetti a disagreeable neighbor. Alex, who had promoted the business, found him particularly offensive. His parties, which lasted sometimes from Thursday nights to Monday mornings (or so it seemed), were loud and occasionally destructive. Twice they had to complain to Lefever about people driving through or parking in their yard.

Alex had finally gone so far as to call the police, secretly hoping that Manetti would be caught with drugs or otherwise illegally engaged and thus stopped. The police had evidently given him a hard time, for Manetti had called up and given a royal cursing to the person who answered the phone. Unfortunately, that person was Dan.

The incident of the police visit and the infamous phone call occurred in late October; it was that event that caused relations among Manetti, Dan and Alex to take a surprising turn.

Alex awoke from a sound sleep the Sunday morning after the Saturday night contretemps. Dan stood by his bed dressed for church. It was his habit to attend the early service at St. Paul's Episcopal.

"Alex, do you have a pair of gloves? Any kind will do." Dan's voice had what Alex later described to friends as a "formal and warlike tone."

Alex sat up, rubbing his eyes. "Sit down, Dan," he mumbled, yawning. Dan continued to stand.

"Do you have any gloves?" he asked again. Alex stared at him for a moment. Then he got out of bed, went over to his dresser, and rummaged around a bit in the bottom drawer. Eventually, he held out two pair: a huge pair of ski gloves and a pair of canvas work gloves that were stained and dirty.

Dan went over and took the work gloves. He turned them over in his hand, eyeing them uncertainly. "These won't do," he said, more to himself than to Alex.

A smile played across Alex's face as he watched Dan solemnly considering the pairs of gloves. "I'm sorry I don't have a wider selection, Dan," he said.

Dan tossed the work gloves onto the dresser. He took one ski glove, fingered it, then said resolutely to himself, "Well, this will have to do." He turned on his heel and left the room, throwing a "Thank you, Alex," over his shoulder.

Dan stood looking after Dan for a few moments, musing on his intent. Then he tossed the other ski glove onto the dresser and followed. Although it was a cool morning, Alex went out onto the porch barefoot, wearing only boxer shorts.

Dan strode across his, then Manetti's lawns. He bounded up onto Jason's porch and rapped loudly and determinedly on the front door.

Manetti answered himself, an unusual occurrence. His sharp, nasal-accented voice was loud enough for Alex to hear clearly. First, he yawned rudely in Dan's face, then said sarcastically, "Well, what the hell do *you* want, Deal?"

Dan replied, but Alex could not hear him.

"Oh, that was *you*?" Manetti said. A laugh. "I'm *so* sorry. Did my language *offend you*?" he asked snidely.

"Yes," Dan said, loudly enough for Alex to hear then something else he couldn't determine.

Suddenly Manetti stiffened. Alex could tell that whatever Dan had said had made him livid. Hands on hips he shouted, "You skinny, half-ass 'Southern gentleman,' I ought to…"

Then something happened. It looked to Alex as if Dan had slapped Jason. Then he realized that Dan had hit Manetti with the ski glove. He was challenging him to a duel.

There was a tableau for a few moments: Manetti, his head cocked, looking at Dan as if he were mad, Dan, standing calmly, looking at Manetti disdainfully.

Manetti began to laugh uproariously. Dan took a step backward as if uncertain what to do. Then, of all things, Manetti stepped forward and threw his arm around Dan's shoulders. The last thing Dan saw was the two of them disappearing into Manetti's house.

Alex shivered and went back into his own home. Musing on what he'd seen, he shaved, showered, and dressed. As he brushed his hair after drying it, Dan came in. He stopped at the open door of Alex's bedroom and proffered the ski glove. Alex noticed that he had three cans of beer, still hanging on a six-pack ring, in his other hand.

"I have had an amazing adventure," Dan said. He gestured with the beers. "Let me put these in the refrigerator and I'll tell you about it."

When Dan returned, Alex invited him out for brunch. Dan almost demurred, citing his natural loathing for change in routine. Then, suddenly, he consented. It was a day for the un-routine, he said.

They were in Alex's Celica on the way to the Village Tavern when Dan began his story. "I borrowed the glove to challenge Manetti to a fight," he said.

Alex looked at him and nodded, his conjecture confirmed.

"It was a bit of a joke, of course," Dan continued, "and it became more of one with the glove you loaned me." He smiled wryly at Alex who nodded his head and laughed softly, though whether at Dan or at the situation he could not say.

Alex swallowed his laughter and asked, "Why the altercation, Dan? What brought out the *code duello* in you?" He glanced at Dan and smiled, but Dan was staring coolly at the road.

"Manetti called last night. You were in the kitchen fixing popcorn. In a conversation that I found remarkable for both its brevity and vulgarity, he roundly cursed me for having called the police about his party." A revelation struck Dan and he turned to Alex slowly. "*You* called the police, didn't you, Alex?"

Dan returned his gaze to the street, musing. "Of course. You and Manetti have been at it for most of the semester. My guess is that it has something to do with that girl." He looked at Alex's face out of the corner of his eye. When Alex blushed slightly, Dan nodded. "I thought so."

Alex shrugged sheepishly. "I'm sorry to have caused the trouble, Dan. If I had answered the phone, I'd have given him as good as I got."

"What makes you think he didn't get it?" Dan asked coyly. Alex looked over at him and he was smiling. Alex smiled in return. "Simply because I confronted him in gentlemanly fashion–albeit with a ski glove in my hand–doesn't mean I hesitated to speak to him in language he could understand," Dan shifted on the car seat. "I will say this for Manetti. He took my action in good humor. He invited me in, gave me the beer I brought home, and introduced me to a scantily clad, blonde person named Grace who provided me with her phone number."

He reached into the pocket of his sport coat and passed a paper to Alex. "Manetti insisted I call her, but I told him I'd pass the number along to you. He seemed quite pleased by that. He told me repeatedly that I was *okay*."

Alex read the name and number, then slipped the paper into his jacket pocket. "So you are, Dan Deal, so you are."

Alex smiled, rather to himself than at Dan. Then the other girl, the one Manetti had stolen came to mind. He stopped smiling.

* * *

"You know," said Dan as they sat in the restaurant, "I sometimes think about the girl we saw that day I first met Manetti. For the life of me I can't recall her face clearly. I'm usually very good with faces, but I don't think I'd know her if I met her again. You knew her pretty well, didn't you?"

Alex looked up abruptly from his menu, but Dan was innocently studying his, suggesting his comment was not meant mockingly. "Yes, I knew her fairly well," he said evenly, watching Dan.

"Well, I know you were disgruntled even more than I was at her faithlessness. Still, women are as they are, n'est-ce pas? Toujours le même quand on cherche la femme, hein?"

Dan's French was impeccable, his linguistic abilities a gift from his mother. He never missed an opportunity to display his talent.

"I suppose," Alex replied flatly. The waitress came and they gave their orders. After she had poured their coffee, Alex said gently, looking out the window, "She was... is, I suppose, a remarkable woman."

"Who's that?" Dan asked affably. "The one we were just talking about?"

"Yes." Alex looked at him and smiled sadly.

Dan nodded solemnly, more out of polite deference to Alex that for any other reason. The waitress brought their food. Alex, to get his mind off Evelyn, introduced another subject. Dan picked up the thread of conversation and they had a pleasant meal, then went home to their books.

Alex pulled Dan away from his studies in the late afternoon to watch a football game but couldn't get himself interested. He kept thinking of the girl, Evelyn. Dan didn't follow the game very well, either. He found himself thinking of the girl he'd talked with Alex about earlier. Try as he might, he couldn't recall her features from the brief glimpse he'd had of her as she turned to flee to the bathroom.

V

The semester wound down. December brought a flurry of activity, the feverish writing of final opinions and briefs. Dan and Alex finished their semesters on the same afternoon, then went home and slept for fifteen hours, trying to make up for weeks of lost rest.

There had been some respites. Jason Manetti had invited them to each of his weekly parties. Alex, in spite of his disaffection with Manetti over Evelyn, attended, at least for a short time, each debauch. Dan, ever the diligent scholar, had gone to only one party, a brief, hedonistic fling before leaving for home Thanksgiving Eve.

Alex had contacted the blonde Grace. She happened to be a junior at Salem College, most attractive, and acquiescent to even his more exotic suggestions.

When he awoke at eleven the morning after his semester was done, he called her to confirm their latest assignation, a date during which they would attend (at least for a time) Manetti's end-of-semester party. They were chatting suggestively when a knock at the door forced Alex to end their conversation because he was unable to shout Dan into action.

It was Manetti. He had, of all things, a Christmas card for Dan and Alex. He also wanted to invite Dan personally to come to his party.

"Tell him he's got to come, Radford," Jason said, flopping on the sofa.

"I'll tell him but I doubt he'll come. He said something about going home tonight. His cousin will be getting in from William and Mary. They're very close. Like brother and sister, I gather."

Alex went and closed the front door. Manetti had simply walked into the room and made himself at home. Dan would have been amazed, Alex thought, smiling wryly.

"There must be some other reason he's going home," said Manetti, musing aloud. He snapped his fingers and sprang up from the sofa. "That's it." He turned to Alex. "Tell him he's got to come, tonight, Radford. Tell him I've fixed him up with a girl.

Something special; sexy and intellectual at the same time. You know, his type."

Alex had moved across the room and was idly poking at the ashes in the fireplace. "Jason," he said, turning to Manetti, "why are you trying to be so nice to Dan? It's not your style."

Manetti snorted, then grinned. He sat again, throwing his legs over the arm of the sofa. "Well, Radford, I'll tell you," he said, lying back, hands behind his head. "Deal's got something. It's like style, except it's not that. You can learn style. I've got that."

Alex turned and looked into the fireplace to keep from laughing in Manetti's face. "Well, Jason, what do you mean, then?" he asked.

"What Deal's got," Manetti continued, "what *you've* got, too, you..." Manetti caught himself. He wondered if these Southern bastards with their manners were rubbing off on him. "What you guys have got can't be learned. It's like it was born in you or something." He sat up and stroked his unshaven chin.

"Perhaps you mean breeding," Alex offered facetiously over his shoulder. He crumpled paper, tossed kindling onto it, then struck a match to light a fire.

"Yeah. That's it. Breeding. Breeding. Christ, that's it exactly. You and Deal. That's what you've got, Radford. Like Englishmen or something. Jesus, yes. Breeding."

Alex stood and brushed his hands after laying a piece of firewood on the blazing kindling. "Yes, that would be it," he said dryly. He checked his watch. "I promised to wake Dan before noon, and it's nearly that now. Do you want to stay and talk with him?"

He was tired of Manetti. Without his parties, women, and money, he was boring.

Manetti leapt to his feet. "Hell, no, I've got a shitload to do to get this party going." He went to the door and opened it himself before Alex could cross the room. "You talk to Deal. Tell him about the girl."

Then to himself, but audibly, "Hell, I've got to get a woman for him. Sexy but classy." He looked grave for a few moments, then broke into a wicked grin. "I know somebody," he said aloud.

He punched Alex, who had followed him to the door, lightly on the arm. "See you, Radford." He sauntered out the door and across the yard, flipping his hand in a final gesture of farewell as he jumped off Alex's porch. Alex watched him until he reached his own lawn, then closed the door gently.

He stood there, hand on doorknob, thinking, for several minutes. Having attended a number of Manetti's parties, he doubted whether any of the girls he'd met there would suit Dan Deal. Still, it might do Dan good to debauch a little after an arduous semester. *What the hell, he thought. I'll ask Dan. He can make his own decision.*

Halfway across the living room it struck whom Jason intended to invite as a date for Dan. He stopped and caught his breath, surprised at his own reaction. He almost decided not to tell Dan of Manetti's invitation. Then he flexed his shoulders and went to wake his friend. He tried to think of Grace. He couldn't hold her in his mind. She kept transforming into Evelyn.

VI

To Alex's surprise (and a bit to his dismay), Dan readily accepted Manetti's invitation. They spent the afternoon prepping for the party by watching a meaningless football game on television and sipping beer. It might be more accurate to say that Dan sipped beer while Alex, rather glum, drank. He had five beers; Dan, only two. After the game, Dan took Alex to Ryan's, a swank local eatery, for dinner. He had planned the outing as Alex's Christmas present; he now also hoped to dispel his usually cheerful friend's air of melancholy.

Dan was in a very good humor. The semester was behind him. Christmas, Grandfather, Cousin Ramona, and perhaps Alicia Pauls lay before. The future looked merry and bright.

Gradually, the administration of an excellent Caesar salad, a perfectly prepared medium rare ribeye steak, a very good baked potato with sour cream and fresh chives, and several glasses of a most potable nouveaux Beaujolais Villages restored a good measure of Alex's Christmas cheer. He was even able to tease Dan a little about his date.

"Manetti said he'd have a girl for you who was both sexy and brainy. That should be some trick for him." Alex smiled and turned his wineglass slowly by its stem, then sipped from it.

"That's rather chauvinistic, Alex," Dan said. "You seem to think there are no such women." He thought of his cousin Ramona and suddenly had an uneasy feeling about Alex. "You may be right, however." He smiled back at his friend.

Alex drained his glass. He made a wry face, perhaps because of the wine's bite, and said, "I'm sure there are such women, Daniel. I just hate to think of Jason Manetti knowing them. He shook his head and looked across the restaurant. "Especially Biblically," he added absently.

Dan chuckled, but Alex's face remained serious for longer than Dan found comfortable. Just as his own smile faded, Alex's broke through. "Well, at least she'll probably be beautiful," he said, looking at Dan. "Manetti seems able to attract the attractive."

Dan poured more wine into Alex's glass, then into his own. He thought of Alicia Pauls. Lovely, blonde Alicia Pauls. Delightful, acquiescent Alicia Pauls. Sensuous, meaningless Alicia Pauls. If Manetti provided someone like Alicia Pauls, the evening could be worthwhile.

Alex held up his glass suddenly. "Merry Christmas, Daniel Randolph Deal," he said.

"Merry Christmas, Wythe Alexander Radford." Dan clinked his glass against Alex's. They drank off the wine and set down their glasses. For several moments they sat and regarded each other; each wondering what the evening might hold. Then, as if on cue, they called for the waitress at the same time. Laughing, Dan paid the bill and they left the restaurant.

The party was in full roar by the time they got home. Not only were Manetti's drive and yard filled with cars, Dan's and Alex's drive (and yard), were filled, too. Dan had to park on the street half a block away.

As they approached Manetti's house, they could hear his stereo blaring at what must surely be maximum volume. The music, barely recognizable as Fleetwood Mac, roared somewhat incomprehensibly amid the shouts and laughter. Even though the night was cold, the front door stood mostly open.

Dan stepped through the doorway into the hot, crowded, smoky room. A petite brunette, whom he recognized for some reason as a Wake Forest cheerleader, held a mug emblazoned with the school's insignia up to his face. An overpowering smell of bourbon and cola assailed his nostrils.

"No, thank you," he said. He smiled politely and tried to pass.

She grabbed the lapel of his overcoat and pulled him down toward her. "Who are you?" she slurred, attempting, he thought, to sound seductive. Alex passed behind him, slipping into the room and giving Dan a pat on the back as he passed. Dan turned his head far enough to catch Alex's wink and wry smile.

He freed his lapel from her fingers and straightened. "My name is Daniel Randolph Deal. Of Lynchburg, Virginia," he said in his most courtly tone.

He still held her hand. He raised her fingers to his lips and kissed them, gently. When he let her hand go, she stood transfixed, her hand still dangling in front of him.

"I'm a law student here at the university," he said, continuing the conversation. She said nothing: she merely lowered her hand slowly and continued staring at him. "I'm a neighbor of Jason Manetti's," he added.

Suddenly Manetti was at his side. "Hey, Deal, you trying to steal my date?" he said, slightly drunkenly it seemed, throwing his arm around Dan's shoulder. He grabbed the girl by the wrist and pulled her to him, then squeezed her shoulders in a hug that made her spill some of her drink.

"Don't worry about it, baby," Manetti growled. "I'll get the maid service in here over the holidays for a major overhaul." Then he kissed her full on the mouth, pulling himself away just as she began to respond in earnest.

"Hey," he said, "I've got you a baby doll around here somewhere, Deal. Let's go find her." He whispered something to the cheerleader and grabbed Dan by the arm to lead him through the crowd.

Dan looked back at the girl as he struggled along behind Manetti. "I'm Terri," she mouthed. She gave her last name, but Dan didn't get it. "Call me," he read from her lips before he turned and followed Manetti willingly. He was trying to figure out what she'd said her last name was when he found himself face to face with another woman.

"Here he is, babe," Dan heard Manetti say from somewhere off to his right. " Mr. Classy himself." Dan felt himself slapped on the back. "Enjoy yourself, Deal. I've got business to attend to."

Dan turned to ask Manetti if he were going to introduce the young lady, but his host was gone through the crowd. He turned back to his new acquaintance. Some people passed by on their way to the kitchen and she stepped closer.

She was lovely. Her hair was a rich auburn, newly cut in the classic pageboy style. Her eyes were, for all practical purposes in the available light, violet. Her complexion was very fair.

"Are your ancestors Irish or Scottish?" Dan asked, no real purpose in his question.

She looked at him and Dan realized that some women, no matter what their pasts, look perpetually innocent. Each new man is her knight in shining armor. Dan felt that when she looked at him. He was utterly disarmed by it.

"No, Belgian," she said, smiling shyly. "And English."

"Ah." Dan could think of nothing else to say immediately.

"Are you from Tidewater Virginia?" she asked. "Your accent sounds like it."

"Not myself. My grandfather is. He brought me up, so I suppose I got my accent from him. I'm from Lynchburg." He smiled nervously.

"Oh." A pause. She looked away, then back at him quickly, a maneuver she looked very beautiful performing. "I have relatives in Virginia."

Dan nodded pointlessly. "Really? Where?" He felt very strongly the desire to lean over and kiss her, and he felt, equally strongly, that she wanted him to. It seemed essential to continue the conversation before he did something foolish.

"Danville," she whispered, stepping even closer to him as another group of people passed.

"I... I went to U.V.A. with some fellows from Danville," he said gently, her mouth only inches away. "One was–ah–Don Scarsdale."

"Oh, I know him." She smiled brightly. "He and my cousin Mitch Milton went to high school together. They still hang out even though Mitch went to Virginia Tech." She wrinkled her nose as she mentioned V. P. I.

Dan ignored her seemingly slighting reference to his father's alma mater. "Mitch Milton?" he asked eagerly.

"Why, yes. Do you know him?" She leaned toward him. Her breath grazed his lips.

"Certainly." Dan swallowed hard. "I met him when he came up to U.V.A. for visits. And when I went home with Don for a couple of weekends, we spent considerable time with Mitch." Dan felt tremendously excited to know her cousin.

"What's your name?" she asked suddenly.

"Dan Deal. Yours?"

"Evelyn. Evelyn Daiches."

They smiled broadly at each other as if they had achieved together some long desired mutual goal.

"Where are *you* from, Evelyn?"

"High Point."

"Ah, furniture."

She smiled again. "Yes, as a matter of fact. My father is president of his own furniture company."

Dan nodded interestedly. "My grandfather used to be in the lumber business," he said; glad to be able to draw even an oblique connection between their backgrounds. She was truly lovely.

"He's retired?" she asked, anxious to be thought insightful.

"Yes." Dan found her insight charming.

Someone turned the stereo's volume even louder. A song came on by The Eagles: "One of These Nights." Soon the room was alive with moving bodies. Dan leaned forward and put his mouth to her ear. "Would you like to get out of here?"

She looked up, startled, then realized that he'd meant the suggestion innocently. "Don't you like to dance?" she asked.

"Not in this kind of traffic."

Dan turned her around and steered her into the kitchen. He took half a six-pack from the refrigerator. Evelyn excused herself briefly.

When she returned she had a jacket and gloves. Dan helped her put the jacket on. They slipped out the back door together into the darkness.

"Can you see?" Evelyn asked. She laid her hand on his arm. "I'm a little night blind."

"I can get us around the house." Dan put his other hand on top of hers and they made their way to the front yard where streetlights gave adequate illumination. Dan offered her a beer. Then they made their way up the street past Dan's place toward Polo Road. As they got away from the street light and into relative shadow, Evelyn stopped him.

"Wait a sec. Hold this."

He took her beer. She got something from her coat pocket and put it into her mouth. When she struck a match, Dan saw that it was a marijuana cigarette. She inhaled deeply and held it out to him.

"No thanks. I never do," he said, declining the proffered joint.

She exhaled with a whoosh. "You've never smoked pot?" she asked, incredulous.

"A few times. But I don't now. And I won't."

"Why not?" She took another toke.

He looked at her intently in the darkness, as if to reassure himself that she was not trying to trick him into saying something that could later be used against him.

37

"There are two good reasons, actually," he said finally. "One, it's an expensive habit. Two, it's illegal. I don't want to try to become a lawyer with a drug conviction on my record."

She nodded and exhaled. "Well, I don't think I'll do it forever. But right now it's okay." As she toked again, a police car turned onto the street where they stood. Dan took the joint from her and tossed it away. The police car stopped as it reached them.

"You people from the party?" The officer gestured toward Manetti's house.

"Yes sir." Chagrined, Dan realized they were holding open alcoholic beverages.

"Be good if you found your way back there," the officer said. "Public street's no place for that." He pointed at the beer cans.

"No sir," Dan replied, relieved.

The police continued down the street, slowing as they passed Manetti's, but continuing on. Evelyn took Dan's arm. "You're very gallant. I could have been in real trouble."

Dan bowed slightly. "Thank you, ma'am. I was afraid you'd be upset."

"Not at all." She paused a moment, then looked earnest. "You're so different from Jason. How do you two get on?"

"Not very well, I'm afraid." Dan started them moving again.

"That's a shame. Sort of." She stopped suddenly and pointed. "What's that?"

Underneath the trees at the back of Manetti's yard were a couple on a blanket. One could dimly make out the glimmer of the man's buttocks as he moved on the woman. "That, my dear," Dan said, amused, "is copulation."

"Good Lord, out here in the cold?" Evelyn shivered.

"They don't seem to be noticing. I'd better warn them about the police." Dan started toward them.

Evelyn held him back. "They'll get mad."

Dan tugged free. "I'm sure they'd rather be mad than arrested. Wait here." He left her at the back steps and crossed the yard quickly, stopping at what he considered a respectful distance. "Uh, I say there," he called hoarsely.

The couple froze. Dan heard murmurs. Then the man rose to a kneeling position, holding his pants in front of him. It was Manetti. "What the hell do you want, Deal?" he growled.

"The police are cruising this block," Dan said coldly. "You'd best watch out."

"Oh." Manetti looked around sheepishly. "Thanks. Man."

Dan turned stiffly and stalked back to the house. "He heard the woman's voice say "police" in a frightened tone. He recognized it as the voice of the cheerleader he'd met earlier.

"Who was it?" asked Evelyn as Dan pushed her up the steps to the back door. She hoped Dan would tell her what she already knew from the indistinct conversation she'd heard.

Dan glanced back across the yard. They had resumed. He adopted his best courtroom technique. "Just a couple of partiers," he said.

Evelyn felt a twinge of disappointment in him. He was just another man, after all.

They went into the house.

VII

Late that night, actually morning at two A.M., the partygoers had all but disappeared. Evelyn and Dan walked slowly up the street toward Dan's car. He'd invited her out for breakfast before taking her home. They'd spent the evening after returning from their walk talking quietly in a corner of the kitchen.

Alex and Grace had come into the kitchen at one point and Dan had called them over. They hadn't stayed long. Alex had appeared ill at ease, glancing first at Dan, then at Evelyn, then at Grace in rapid succession again and again, then grabbing at the first opportunity to separate and "get back to the party" as he'd put it.

Dan had the faint impression that Alex and Evelyn knew each other, but she'd seemed completely indifferent to him, focusing all her warmth on Dan. She so intoxicated him that between her and the beer they'd drunk he soon forgot about Alex, the party, even going home to Lynchburg.

As they reached his car, Evelyn gave a low whistle. Dan glanced at her, surprised. An adage of his grandfather's, often quoted to his cousin Ramona, came to mind: "Whistling girls and crowing hens/ Always come to some bad end."

"I take it you like my car," he said, smiling slightly.

Evelyn looked at him. He had looks, intelligence, boyish charm, a nice enough body. That he might be rich seemed almost too much. "You must be rich," she said, rubbing her hand caressingly on the roof of the car as Dan unlocked her door.

Dan leaned over her once she was in the car. "Not rich," he said, grinning slyly. "But not poor."

She reached up, put her hand behind his head, and kissed him. Deeply. For a full minute. When they broke apart, both were a bit breathless.

'Do we have to go out?" Evelyn asked, touching first the corner of her mouth, then of his.

Dan looked surprised. "You'd rather... I took you back... to your dorm?"

41

Evelyn lowered her eyes, then looked back at him for full effect. "I thought perhaps we could... have something at your place."

Dan understood her perfectly. "Of course," he said. He stepped back and closed her door gently. As he walked around to his side of the car, he wondered if he and Alex had anything to eat in the house. He wondered if it mattered.

It took only moments to drive down the street to his house. Evelyn complimented the Porsche's performance. He promised her a long ride some time.

When they arrived at the house and got inside, an array of clothing–male and female–lay scattered on the sofa and floor. "Well. I take it Alex and his friend Grace are already here," Dan observed dryly. Evelyn bit her lip.

At that moment Alex stepped into the living room wearing nothing but a bathrobe. "Dan, I..." He began, faltering when he saw Evelyn.

"Hello, Alex," Dan said teasingly. "You know Evelyn, don't you?"

"Yes," Alex replied flatly.

No one spoke for several moments. Dan took Evelyn's arm and, as he pulled her toward the kitchen, said, "We're going to make ourselves a snack, Alex. Ah, I see you've had a fire. Poke it to life if you would, please. Would you and..." he stopped in the doorway to the kitchen and turned, blocking Evelyn off, "Grace like some coffee or a sandwich?"

Alex began picking up items of clothing from the sofa. "Yes. Some coffee would be nice. I'll come and get us some after I've..." He gestured first toward his room, then at the fire.

"Of course." Dan smiled graciously, then turned and propelled himself and Evelyn into the kitchen. Busily, noisily, they made toasted cheese sandwiches and coffee. As Evelyn prepared to pour coffee into mugs, Dan took down a bottle from the cabinet and poured some into each cup. "Homemade apple brandy," he explained. "To keep the chill away, as my grandfather would say." He smiled facetiously.

Evelyn put down the coffeepot. "I was counting on you to do that," she said, drawing him to her. When they looked up from their kiss, Grace, dressed in Alex's robe, stood shyly watching them.

"I came to get coffee for Alex and myself," she said softly.

Dan watched her quietly. Her blonde beauty and state of undress sharply reminded him of Alicia Pauls.

Evelyn responded smoothly, putting two sandwiches on a plate for her and helping her to arrange that with two cups of coffee on a tray so that she could carry it all back to Alex.

"Compliments of the kitchen of Chez Daniel," she said with a smile and wink as she handed the tray to Grace. Grace thanked her shyly.

Evelyn looked askance at Dan as Grace padded from the room. He seemed to be far away. He stood thoughtfully twisting the cap on his bottle of brandy. She picked up the coffeepot and poured coffee into the remaining cups, then took the bottle from Dan and added a generous dose of brandy into each.

She closed the bottle, put it on the counter, handed Dan the plate of sandwiches, and led the way into the living room carrying the coffee cups before her. She motioned with her head for Dan to follow.

Instead of sitting on the sofa, they made a pallet on the floor in front of the fireplace. Dan stirred the fire and added wood. Soon it was crackling nicely. For a time they were silent, nibbling at their sandwiches, looking at each other occasionally and smiling.

Suddenly Dan tossed off his coffee, then went first to his room, Evelyn guessed by the sound, afterwards to the kitchen. He returned with a book under his arm, the coffeepot in one hand, brandy bottle in the other. After making himself another drink and freshening Evelyn's, he opened the book, an edition of Yeats' poems, and, "bending down beside the glowing bars," read to her.

As he finished "A Deep Sworn Vow," she laid her hand on the open pages.

"Could you love me, Dan?" she asked softly.

He moved her hand and read, "He wishes for the Cloths of Heaven."

"I think I could love you," she said.

He looked at her wistfully. She leaned towards him and held out her hands. "Come. Let's go make love."

He sat motionless.

She got to her feet, picked up her shoes, and padded back to his bedroom. He heard the clicking as the door opened, then closed behind her.

He closed the book and patted it against his hand. He thought about his obligations: to Ramona, to Alicia Pauls, to his grandfather. Thinking about his grandfather brought to mind one of the old gentleman's favorite saws: A gentleman should always try to please a lady in whatever she asks. He felt that explained what he ought to do.

His room was dark when he opened the door. "Evelyn?" he said softly.

No response.

He undressed, then walked around the bed to open the window by its head.

"Don't," she said. "It'll be too cold."

Dan liked to sleep with a window slightly open, no matter the weather. He paused a few moments. He felt compromising his regular habits would violate the gentlemanly principle of discipline, but he also felt that as a gentleman he should give the lady's wishes every consideration. He concluded that something done out of consideration of a lady's wishes could not be thought compromise.

There was another window on the adjacent wall just beyond the foot of the bed. He lowered the window by the head of his bed and opened the other one.

When he climbed into the bed, Evelyn slid against him. "Thank you for lowering the window," she said.

"You're welcome." He gently laid his hand on the inside of her thigh and she crooked her knee to put her right leg on his left. "Won't your roommate wonder where you are?" he asked suddenly.

She caught a quick breath in response to the maneuverings of his hand. "Are you afraid we'll get into trouble?" She bit his ear lobe lightly.

"No."

A pause.

"Are you sleepy?" Evelyn asked.

"Hardly." Dan smiled in the darkness.

"Let's stay awake then." Her voice was coy.

"If you like." His voice tried for courtly, stopped at breathless.

"I'd like to very much."

The rest of the conversation was not of a public nature.

VIII

Dan left Winston-Salem Saturday afternoon. He had taken Evelyn to brunch, then to her dorm. By the time he returned to the house, Alex had his car packed and was ready to leave. Their farewell was rather fragmented, Dan preoccupied by memories of the previous evening, Alex tentative, almost shy on that subject, especially when Dan asked him if he knew Evelyn. Alex realized early in their talk that Dan had not recognized Evelyn as the girl at Manetti's that summer morning; the one he (Alex) had thought he could fall in love with.

"Are you–ah–inviting Evelyn to your house over the holidays?" Alex asked as he watched Dan toss clothes into suitcases and a laundry bag.

Surprised, Dan turned to him. "I hadn't even thought of it, Alex. We've only just met." It occurred to Dan then that he and Evelyn had meant to exchange home phone numbers but had forgotten to.

"Oh." Alex glanced about the room, at a loss to continue the conversation. He thought about Grace, then Evelyn pushed her from his mind. She was always doing that.

"Are you having Grace up to Lightfoot?" Dan asked, breaking into his friend's reverie.

Alex sat down on the bed beside Dan's suitcases and studied his hands. "Yes. Yes, I am. Grace is coming for a couple of days between Christmas and New Year. Probably the twenty-seventh and twenty-eighth."

Dan closed one of his suitcases and snapped it shut. "Then it's going well for you two, I take it?" he said, straightening up and looking at Alex.

Alex glanced up at him. He wanted to stand up and punch Dan as hard as he could in the face. Over a damned capricious woman. Then for some odd reason, he thought of Winnie-the-Pooh. *Silly Old Dan* crossed his mind. *Good old Dan. Ever the gentleman.* "All right, I guess," he said at last.

Dan went to his closet and took out a couple of sport coats. He put those into a suit bag, then tried to close his other suitcase. He had some trouble getting it closed, so Alex moved over and sat

45

on it while Dan snapped it shut. "That should weigh a ton," he said as Alex got to his feet beside him.

"True." They looked at each other, then smiled self-consciously. "Have a Merry Christmas, Dan," Alex said sincerely, holding out his hand.

"Merry Christmas, Alex." They shook hands firmly. Suddenly both burst out laughing. "Lefever," Dan managed to say finally.

Alex helped Dan carry his things out to the Porsche. They shook hands again as they stood between their cars. "I'll call you after Christmas. Perhaps you can come spend New Year's Eve and the weekend after with us," Dan said.

"I'll try. Usually there's a good bit going on with my friends around Williamsburg and Norfolk. Perhaps not for New Year's Eve, but for that following weekend."

"That'll be fine." Dan went around his car and opened the door. "Have a safe trip home, Alex."

"Same to you. Merry Christmas."

"Merry Christmas."

They got into their cars and headed home for whatever the holidays might bring.

IX

Dan got to Lynchburg about six-thirty. He got past the explanation to his grandfather about his late arrival as best he could, then proceeded to enjoy his holiday. He thought about Evelyn, but not unduly much. He tried to maintain perspective.

He knew he had a propensity for romanticizing his relationships with women, probably, he thought, a result of having grown up without his mother. He realized that he and Evelyn had only had a night together. He realized, nonetheless, that it had been a special night.

Had Alicia Pauls not called, he might have weakened enough to try to reach Evelyn. Alicia helped him to maintain perspective. Actually, he maintained perspective well enough to have spent the night of December twenty-third wrapped in a couple of quilts with Alicia in his grandfather's cabin on the remaining family farm about ten miles northwest of Lynchburg.

At one point during the night, while Alicia slept quietly beside him and he wondered whether his story to his grandfather about staying with a buddy at the cabin so as to get an early bird hunt in before returning to Lynchburg for last minute shopping was believed, he got up and went to the cabin's window to watch the cold December moon. He considered his situation.

Many of his friends had maintained the same kinds of liaisons, sexual relationships that continued regularly over an extended period. Usually these relationships began in high school and ended some time around the close of the male's college career. Dan had been tardy in establishing his relationship, and it had lasted longer than most.

He had first slept with Alicia during his freshman year at U.V.A. She had attended Longwood College for a year but had dropped out and taken the secretarial science course at Lynchburg Community College. She had been a set-up, the only blind date he'd ever had.

He had never talked seriously to her of commitment, and she had never hinted that he should. She had seriously dated an insurance salesman for several months, even accepting an

47

engagement ring, but when he'd called from Charlottesville and invited her for a weekend when he was lonely, she had come. By the time he'd come home for summer vacation, the insurance man had disappeared.

Her tender caresses had helped celebrate his victories and assuage his defeats. He wasn't quite sure why he'd turned to her ministrations in his present circumstances.

And now Evelyn complicated matters.

He returned to the bed and slipped gently under the covers. Alicia stirred beside him. Then her hand reached up and lay flat, palm down, on his abdomen. It began to inch lower and he slid closer to her, reaching for her, trying to gain more perspective.

X

On Christmas Eve, Evelyn called.

It was about six o'clock in the evening and Grandfather Deal had just lit the tree.

The entire family was gathered. Gifts were to be exchanged.

Aunt Edith took the call. She whispered to Dan as he stood beside Grandfather watching the twinkling colored lights. "Daniel," she whispered, "telephone for you. It's a young lady. She sounds upset."

Daniel sniffed. It would be Alicia Pauls, upset, probably tipsy, because he'd not invited her to spend Christmas Eve with his family. Again.

Then his aunt surprised him. "It's long distance."

His grandfather took his arm as he turned to go to the phone. "You oughtn't go anywhere tonight."

"I don't plan to, sir."

"Your uncles have a surprise," the old man added, his eyes twinkling, reflecting the Christmas tree lights.

"Yes sir. I'll be right back." He slipped away and hurried to the phone. "Hello?" he said tentatively.

"Is this Dan Deal?"

"Yes. Who is this?" He thought he knew.

"Evelyn."

She didn't have to say Evelyn who. "How did you get my number?" was the first thing he could think of to say.

"Don Scarsdale. My cousin Mitch called him for me."

"Oh."

"Are you surprised to hear from me?" she asked uncertainly. She thought perhaps she'd erred in calling him and not calling Alex Radford.

"Rather, yes." That sounded wrong to him, so he amended. "I suppose I mean tonight. Christmas Eve."

"Oh." A pause. "I hope I'm not disturbing anything important," she said insincerely.

"Why are you calling, Evelyn?" He didn't want to be rude, but he didn't intend to make his grandfather wait too long.

49

"To say Merry Christmas, Dan Deal." Her voice suggested hurt feelings.

"Merry Christmas, Evelyn," he replied gently. "Was there anything else?" he asked quietly.

The conversation took a ludicrous turn.

"Yes, there was something else," she said.

"What?" He tried to sound cheery, but he was becoming testy. He needed to get her off the phone and get back to his family.

"Could you come to see me?"

"When?"

"Now." Her voice broke. She sounded as if she actually meant it.

"Evelyn, what night is this, dear?" he asked patiently.

"Christmas Eve." She sniffled softly.

"Why aren't you with your family?"

He heard a shuddering sigh through the telephone line. "They're at my aunt's. Right next door. I said I'd come later. But I don't want to go there. I want to be with you." She broke down again.

He cleared his throat. "Well," he said, trying to be firm and gentle at once, "all of my relatives are here at my grandfather's house."

"Oh. So I am disturbing you." She sighed again, another shudder.

"Yes and no."

Silence

"Yes, literally you are disturbing me at this gathering. No, I don't mind being disturbed. Yes, it disturbs me that you're calling me. No, I don't mind that disturbance, either."

"I don't understand," she said.

Dan sighed. "Neither do I." He felt then as if he'd made a misstep, been drawn into something, said too much.

"Could you come to see me?" she asked again, coyly, sure now that he would because of what he'd just said.

"When?" he asked again.

"Now," she said to be difficult.

"Not now." He sighed.

"Soon?"

"Soon."

"When soon?"

"Right after Christmas."

"When right after Christmas?"

Dan sighed again, worn down by her maneuvering. "December twenty-sixth." He regretted his words immediately.

"Can you get to High Point?"

"Yes."

"Can you get to my house?"

"No."

"I'll explain." After three minutes of unclear directions he made a suggestion. "Why don't you meet me somewhere and lead me back to your place?"

"That's a good idea, Dan Deal. I'll meet you at the Shell station by the Highway 311 exit. About noon. Okay?"

In spite of his inclination to back out, Dan heard himself say, "Fine."

Silence.

"Was there anything else?" he asked.

"Will you spend the night?" she whispered.

"No," he said, too firmly.

Another silence.

"Anything else?" He asked, too gently.

"Thank you, Dan Deal. I know I've been a bother. You've been a perfect gentleman."

Dan thought he detected the faintest hint of sarcasm in her tone. "No bother," he said. "You're quite welcome. And thank you for the compliment," he added, testing to see if she were sarcastic.

She wasn't sure she understood what compliment he referred to, then realized he'd taken her gentleman comment seriously. "You're welcome," she said warmly to throw him off the scent. "Goodbye, Dan. Merry Christmas."

"Goodbye, Evelyn. Merry Christmas."

Then she was gone. He sat by the phone for a few minutes trying to sort through it all, but it was too soon yet for that. He went back to the gathering but found himself distracted by thoughts of her. His grandfather actually had to remind him to thank his cousin Ramona for her gift of a cashmere sweater he'd admired.

Then came the promised surprise. Dan's uncles, his father's brothers, had always been most generous to him. This occasion was no exception. Each uncle presented him with an expensive suit, Uncle Charles a navy blue, Uncle Arthur and Aunt Edith, a gray pinstripe.

"You'll look mighty fine in those," Grandfather said, more excited than Dan.

"Yes sir, I will."

"We thought you might need those for your summer job," Uncle Charles added dryly, a twinkle in his eye.

"Sir?" Dan was genuinely surprised. He knew nothing of any summer job.

"We've arranged for you to clerk at Willis and Boatwright." Uncle Arthur leaned back on the sofa beside Aunt Edith and smiled. He appeared to Dan like a latter day version of his favorite picture of his father, one that stood on his grandfather's desk in the den. A lawyer himself, Arthur Deal had chosen to partner his brother in the general contracting firm that kept the family a fair distance from poverty and provided Grandfather Deal with the expensive Madeira of which he was so fond.

Dan was momentarily speechless. His uncles had arranged a summer job for him with the most prestigious law firm in western Virginia, virtually assuring him an excellent entry-level post with almost any Virginia law firm after his graduation. As his grandfather was about to upbraid him for forgetting his manners twice in one evening, he thanked his aunt and uncles as effusively as his and their reserved natures would allow.

Long after everyone had gone home and Grandfather Deal had gone to bed, Dan lingered in the living room. Sitting on the sofa, the tree lights glimmering, he sat considering the suits his uncles had given him and musing about the prestigious clerking opportunity they'd arranged. Their largess never failed to move him.

It would have been easy for them to resent him, he felt, because his father, the oldest brother, had also been Grandfather's favorite. They had never expressed any feelings except love and kindness toward him. He drew his fingertips across the sleeve of the blue suit and wondered if he were the only Deal with base traits in his temperament.

He thought of Alicia Pauls. He had meant to call her but had forgotten. The resolve to end that relationship and allow her to go on with her life came to him as a fine, glowing feeling of peace.

The clock chimed twelve. Christmas. He felt a momentary pang of regret at having declined his uncles' invitation to join them in attending the midnight service at St. Bartholomew's Episcopal Church.

Then Evelyn came to him in a thought so real, so sensuous, that he felt himself stirred. When the thought passed, he laughed softly, almost in relief. He tried to think of her again but felt unable to.

In the quiet a log in the fireplace slipped and crackled. He could hear the hall clock tick. Gifted generously, righteously resolved, he felt at peace.

XI

Christmas Day came and went, as too often happens when one is adult and alone, anticlimactically. For Dan, the day felt strange, rather like a second Christmas Eve, full of continued expectation.

The family met at Aunt Edith and Uncle Arthur's home. There was bountiful fare and Grandfather Deal drank a bit too much Madeira, both family customs. As evening came on, the first snow of the winter fell. It was very little, only a whitening of the ground, although the sky was quite gray and it was cold for December.

Just as the snow began, Dan took his cousin Ramona for a walk. As the only offspring of the Deal family, they had always been unusually close. Uncle Charles' confirmed bachelor status cemented their familial posts. They served the triple functions of being only children, only grandchildren, and only niece and nephew.

Although Aunt Edith insisted there could be no sibling competition between cousins, both Dan and Ramona knew otherwise. Dan was attractive and gentlemanly with considerable intellect and a sort of innocuous charm. Ramona was a stunning beauty possessed with a wit and frankness that both attracted and intimidated boys and men. Dan was blond and blue eyed like his mother; Ramona had the dark locks and hazel eyes of the Deal family.

In high school their differences could not have been more obvious: Dan's charming reticence and seeming intellectual invulnerability secured him the presidency of his school's chapter of the National Honor Society; Ramona's beauty and wit got her elected both homecoming queen and senior class president. It was always a source of mild discontent to Dan that the family viewed their achievements as equally golden.

At one point, during his junior year at U.V.A., in the midst of reading heavily in Byron, Dan resolved to seduce his cousin. She was a senior in high school and had just been named homecoming queen. Promising Aunt Edith and Uncle Arthur that he would find a suitable place for her to spend the night, he took her down to Charlottesville.

They watched the football game, which Virginia won, a rarity then, amid an admiring crowd of Dan's fraternity brothers, sharing a flask of coffee laced with brandy to ward off the November chill. After the game and a delightful dinner with two of Dan's friends and their dates, they spent the required number of hours at the fraternity bash.

By two A. M. they were both tired and a bit tipsy. It was then that Dan suggested they retire for the evening. Ramona was reluctant to desert the merriment, but Dan, his air affectedly mysterious and Byronic, hinted that there might be even more thrills when they were alone. She eyed him interestedly and followed him to his car.

He drove her to a small house just outside Charlottesville about a quarter mile off the highway. It belonged to one of Dan's former fraternity brothers who was currently attending the law school. He was away for the weekend and Dan had arranged to use his little hideaway. Surrounded by towering pines and bounded at the back by a rushing stream, it seemed an appropriately Romantic place for a seduction.

As they relaxed on the sofa, a bottle of chilled *liebfraumilch* for company, Joni Mitchell crooning softly from the stereo, Dan took a strategically placed volume of poetry from the coffee table and read, first from Canto III of *Childe Harold's Pilgrimage*, then from Canto II of *Don Juan*.

As he read of Juan and Haidee's love affair, Ramona slipped closer and closer to him so that when he looked up after reading, 'Their lips drew near and clung into a kiss,' her face was barely two inches from his own. She took the book from him, tossed it aside, and drew him down onto her on the sofa.

They kissed, a long, long kiss. When it ended, while Dan nuzzled her throat and began gently unbuttoning her blouse, she asked him softly, "Dan, are you going to make love to me?"

He stopped nuzzling and raised himself so as to look down at her. "That's why I brought you here," he whispered breathlessly. His eyes flashed Byronically he hoped.

She gazed up at him calmly. "Then you'd probably better pull out. I went off the pill about two months ago, so I'm unprotected.

Unless, of course, you've got some foam or a condom or something."

He stared at her. She was completely calm. He sat up and leaned back on the sofa, shaking his head. Byron hadn't prepared him for such a sensible, resourceful woman.

Straightening her skirt, Ramona sat up. Dan eyed her askance. His look prompted her to begin explaining herself. "Do you remember Tommy Hengist? He was my boyfriend last year. You know, the football star. The quarterback."

Dan nodded numbly, unsure if he knew the person or not, or if it mattered.

"Well, he was the first. We got really drunk after last year's homecoming game, and he took advantage of me. I couldn't call it rape because I wanted to." She smiled at Dan in a way that made him smile in return, albeit confusedly.

"The next afternoon," she continued, "after I'd spent the whole day in my room, crying my eyes out, feeling guilty as sin, he called me to 'apologize.' He was such a smug bastard that I told him to go to hell and called up Stan Horsa, a big linebacker whom I knew was crazy about me and of whom Tommy was terribly jealous. I dated him that night, we had some beers, and then I did with him what I'd done with Tommy. Somehow I thought I'd show Tommy he wasn't so great. But Stan actually wasn't as good as Tommy." She giggled and Dan's shoulders drooped.

Ramona leaned over and patted Dan's cheek. "Almost done," she said gently, but teasingly. "Anyway, after that weekend the word was out about me, so I spent a few weeks driving off the cretins who wanted to make a full-fledged whore of old Ramona. I finally had to begin dating guys from Roanoke for a while until things settled down just to get some peace… hmm, poor word choice." She smiled mischievously at Dan and he smiled, too, thoroughly whipped.

"Any others?" he asked, he hoped not accusingly.

"One other guy. That was a fling last summer at the beach–just lust–on my part," she added. She leaned over and nipped Dan's ear.

He shrugged away and stared at the blue light emanating from the stereo receiver. "Unbelievable," he said finally.

"Not really. There's only one virgin on the cheer leading squad, and she's a sophomore." She played with the hair on the back of his neck as she talked, looking at it rather than at him. "Maybe you should have asked her up here," she said facetiously.

Dan blushed slightly and was glad for the dimness of the room. He caught her eye and said quietly, "So. You've had three lovers." He shook his head. She was one ahead of him.

She put her fingers to his lips. Then she leaned over and kissed him lightly. "Yes, Dan. Three," she said indulgently. "If you want to call those first two lovers. More like a rooster on a hen."

Dan laughed then and so did she. He got up and went over to change the record. When he came back, he put his feet up on the coffee table and reached up and turned off the lamp beside the sofa. He put his hands behind his head and studied the blue light of the stereo again.

Ramona leaned over and kissed him. She began to take off his tie and unbutton his shirt.

He stopped her. He took hold of her hand and kissed it.

"Très aimable, monsieur," she said.

"Miss Armour's French class, I see." He smiled.

She snuggled against him and drew her feet up onto the sofa. He eased out of his loafers and turned sideways so that they could lie together. Ramona pulled a blanket lying on the back of the sofa down over them and they made themselves comfortable. The night deepened around them.

Late the next morning they set out on the return drive to Lynchburg. They were shy with each other, occasionally holding hands as they drove along together.

Ramona and Dan walked arm in arm through the lightly falling snow. From time to time Dan scuffed at gravel on the sidewalk. Ramona held his arm comfortably, familiarly, as if they were a married couple. "What do you want to talk about?" she asked.

Dan knew better than to quibble about wanting to talk. Ramona knew him too well.

"A girl," he said.

"A woman, you mean?" It was one of Ramona's particular pleasures to tease Dan about his male chauvinism, learned at the knee of their grandfather. It was, she felt, a little sadly, his ignorance of women that would be his downfall. She hoped that he would eventually see that the physical pleasures of relationships were not the end in itself. She wanted him to see her–indeed, all women–as complete beings.

Dan sighed. Ramona was always trying to 'liberate' him from his 'benighted' masculinity. "A woman," he said, acquiescing to her prodding.

"Special?" The edge on the word when Ramona said it made Dan glance at her in surprise.

"Maybe." He shrugged noncommittally. "Too early to tell."

"What's her name?" Ramona stopped and looked at one of the monstrous sized Victorian houses they were passing. Perhaps she should get Dan together with Audrey Robinson, she thought. Audrey had carried a torch for him since high school. Better to bear an ill she knew (Audrey was, after all, sweet and pretty) than let him fly to one she knew not of. She wondered if Dan thought much about Charlottesville, about homecoming.

"Evelyn." Dan said the name tentatively, as if pronouncing a new word in French, as if trying it out to see what would happen.

Ramona knew then that she had nothing to fear from Evelyn. "A pretty name," she said. "Is she as pretty as the name?" Perhaps, she thought, it was better to be coy, to treat the matter lightly. Dan had two and a half years of law school left. That was a very long time.

Dan nodded. "I think so," he said firmly. Probably best to be frank with her, he said to himself. Charlottesville was two years gone. After all, he concluded, feeling wise and philosophical, she's my first cousin.

Ramona could think of no way to ask the next question except directly. "Are you sleeping with her?"

He pressed her arm against his and grasped her mitten tightly in his glove. She knew the answer then.

He smiled apologetically. Ramona was as mysterious as the rest of them sometimes. "Funny you should ask."

They stopped at a street corner. After waiting for a car to pass and waving to its occupants–neighbors of Dan's, two aged women who lived by themselves nearby–suddenly Ramona saw herself old and alone.

As they crossed the street and continued their walk, Dan related the events surrounding the party and his becoming involved with Evelyn.

"And you're going to see her tomorrow? To meet her parents?" Evelyn asked, clearly surprised.

Dan did not like the incredulity in Ramona's voice. "Yes," he said shortly.

She smiled an infuriatingly superior smile. "For a Phi Beta Kappa, you can do some amazingly unintelligent things."

She took her arm from his, stopped walking, and stood on tiptoe to peer over the hedge at a large white house similar to her grandfather's.

"That's the Cassidy place," Dan said menacingly. He felt resentment at Ramona's casual condescension toward his decision to go and see Evelyn. He felt proud and decisive in the face of her derision. He *would* go and see Evelyn. She would sing a different tune when he and Evelyn... then he paused. He realized he had no thought of Evelyn as part of his future; short or long term. "Those are the people who bought out Grandfather." His tone was icy. To his mind, Deal money had bought that fine home.

"I know," Ramona said absently, gazing at the house. "I had... almost had an affair with Phil Cassidy this fall. At school." She turned to Dan and waited without looking directly at him. She hoped her hastily added "almost," an addition to spare his ego, worked.

"What?" She smiled at Dan's incredulous tone. She gathered from his tone that he was more concerned with *whom* than *what*, so she knew she was safe. Dan rarely backtracked. Men almost never did.

"Oh," she said casually, taking his arm and starting them moving again, "he took me to some football games. He took me sailing. We dated for a couple of months." She added without thinking, "He's really quite sweet."

"Perhaps time and our money have refined the blood," Dan said acidly.

She knew then she would never tell him that she'd broken off the relationship–hurt Phil badly and caused herself no small pain–because she knew her family would never approve. "You sound like father and Uncle Charles," she said, sighing. She wondered idly why men insisted upon being children their entire lives. Her admiration for her mother grew in that moment. Whether it was Dan's intolerance or Phil's inability to understand, she realized that with men there would always be something to cover, something to ignore.

"We came out here to talk about me, remember? About *my* problem." Dan's voice brought her back to the present circumstance.

Ramona smiled at him, glad to be free of her rumination, pleased to hear the word *problem*. "Oh, yes. Your *problem*. Well, Dan, the solution is simple. Of course, being a man, you can't see it."

"Oh, really." Dan pursed his lips in disdain. He found her indulgent tone irritating. Women always thought they knew the answer to every question.

She stepped back and looked at him earnestly. "You see, Dan, you won't be able to see this girl clearly unless you stay away from her for awhile. Or else, keep your relationship unphysical. Neither of which you'll do. Men never can. Even *gentlemen*. You're slaves of your glands."

"Oh. I see." He smiled at her; this time he was the indulgent one.

She looked away from him, at the ground, realizing that he saw nothing. She thought of telling him the truth about her love affair with Phil Cassidy, of Phil's kindness and courtesy, and of the calculated way she'd hurt him and herself to protect the family.

Perhaps then he'd understand women a little, grasp their calculations, their ability to distance themselves in relationships out of pure practicality, an ability she believed men did not possess. Then maybe he'd reconsider his foolishness over Evelyn. She looked at him. He was looking into the sky in perfect innocence, wondering at the snow as she'd seen him do when they were children. She realized she loved him too much to tell him. He would have to learn that from some other woman.

She shivered and touched his arm. "Let's go back," she said. "I'm cold."

It was beginning to snow harder. She walked away from him so quickly that he had to jog a few steps to catch up to her. He took her arm and slowed her.

On the way back he asked if she were seeing anyone. He was glad to hear that she was not. She'd be willing to meet Alex.

61

"So. No great loves, then?" he asked jovially, glad to put her earnest advice away from him. Sometimes he thought women didn't have a jot of romance in them.

She caught at his tone. "No, none," she said, then added facetiously, "except perhaps Phil Cassidy." She eyed him askance to check his reaction.

They turned in at the sidewalk leading to Ramona's house. Dan knocked the snow from his shoes as they went up onto the porch. "You've not been involved with anyone for a long time... except Phil Cassidy, of course." He smiled to show that he wasn't being mean.

"Except Phil." Her tone made him glad he'd been gentle. She drew him to her and put her arms about his neck.

He slipped his arms around her. "Why?"

She leaned back and looked up at him. He thought about her eyes, a rich greenish blue, which he couldn't see in the darkness.

She leaned forward and laid her lips against his ear. "I'm saving myself," she whispered, giving something away, knowing he'd probably miss it.

He kissed her cheek, then turned away and opened the door for her. Something about what had just happened made him desperate for Grandfather's gaiety.

XII

Weather broadcasts reported the threat of more snow, but December twenty-sixth dawned partly cloudy and cold. Dan convinced his grandfather that the danger was slight, and so the old man gave his grudging consent to Dan's travel plans. As Dan had pointed out, he'd be traveling south, in the direction of warmer climes.

The sky had completely clouded over by the time Dan left Lynchburg at ten that morning. By the time he reached the North Carolina border, the weather had turned foul. He pondered whether to continue or to return home. All the while he moved ever southward, in effect making the decision.

By the time he passed Reidsville, some thirty miles north of High Point, the snow had reached true storm intensity. The wind blew in gusts and snow came at the Porsche's windshield horizontally. Dan pulled the car over beneath an overpass and sat for some minutes hoping that the snow would abate some and allow him to continue at a reasonable pace.

As he sat there he closed his eyes. The purr of the Porsche's idling engine was barely audible in the whirl of wind and hiss of snow. Then, from far off, he thought he heard a woman's voice– his mother's voice, perhaps–or Ramona's. It was calling him back to Virginia, to home, to his own.

He sat up with a start. He must have been dreaming. The snow seemed to have diminished some, so he eased back onto U.S. 29 and moved toward High Point again.

Even as he continued he wondered about his dream. The Biblical story of the child Samuel and how he heard God's voice came to him and he pondered that during the rest of the drive.

XIII

Evelyn was waiting at the service station as arranged when Dan arrived over an hour late. She was glad and surprised to see him. "I was going to call home at two o'clock and tell my brother to come pick me up, and I expected to hear you'd called and said you couldn't make it." She brushed snow from his shoulders as they stood by his car.

"I almost turned around up near Reidsville. But then I decided I couldn't disappoint you." He looked around at the snow-covered scene for a car that might be hers. "Shall I follow you?" he asked.

"I'll ride with you, if that's okay. My brother brought me here because my dad didn't want me to drive in the snow." She shook her head. "Men," she added. "They always assume women need their help."

"Don't they?" Dan asked archly.

She looked up at him in the falling snow and knew him for what he was: another one of them. Still, she was glad to see him. She needed him close to see if she really felt something for him or if he were merely a shield from the temptation of Jason Manetti who'd called three times since she'd been home. "I'm glad to see you," she said softly.

Dan smiled, flattered. "And I, you." With a chivalrous flourish he opened the car door for her.

The drive to Evelyn's house turned out to be a convoluted affair. She lived in an ancient and honorable country club section of the city. They drove slowly through the tree-lined lanes, partly out of respect for the snow on the streets, partly out of Dan's admiration for the homes they passed.

Finally they stopped before an impressive Williamsburg style home with white trim and black shutters. Distrustful of the incline of the drive, they parked on the street.

Mrs. Daiches met them at the door. She was a slender, attractive woman somewhere in her late forties. Dan recognized immediately where Evelyn got her violet eyes. After a hurried introduction and brushing away of snow, they went into the den where Dan met the rest of Evelyn's immediate family.

Mr. Daiches was tall and 'of a port in air' as Dan described him to a literate friend later. In keeping with the holidays he sported red and green plaid slacks, a white oxford cloth shirt and a red cardigan. He held what Dan quickly came to recognize as a perennial drink in his hand.

Evelyn's brother Russ was tall like his father but slender, obviously in excellent shape. Dan immediately pegged him for a tennis player and was gratified when his speculation turned out to be correct. His wife Nicole was a brunette for whom the description smoldering was not a cliché. A look in her gray eyes bespoke, to Dan at least, urgency of some sort.

Evelyn's mother drew Dan into the room and led him to the sofa. "So, Dan. You're a lawyer."

"Actually, a law student, ma'am," Dan corrected. He glanced at Evelyn who had taken a seat next to Nicole on the sofa and hoped she hadn't misled her family.

She caught his look and read the question in it. "I said law school, Mother," she said. She smiled at Dan, the conspiratorial smile of the child who doesn't want to be held responsible for the vagaries of her parents. Having had no parents, Dan could not respond.

"At Wake Forest," Mr. Daiches put in firmly to show that *he* was not mistaken in *his* information.

"Yes sir."

"Do you have a particular area you're going to specialize in?" Nicole asked, wrapping her fingers languidly around a cup of what Dan discovered moments later when Mrs. Daiches served him, was mulled wine, and catching him in her gaze.

"I'm very interested in contracts," Dan said steadily, unable to break away from her regard.

"I'm interested in the law myself," she said, then sipped her punch and looked at the fireplace, freeing Dan. He looked for Evelyn who had gone over to the stereo to change the Christmas music to Sinatra. Nicole then continued, drawing Dan's attention to her again, "Russ says I can start law school next year. If I'm not pregnant," she added, dropping her voice pitch even lower, her gray eyes lingering on him for a beat more than he thought necessary or proper, then moving to Russ who scowled and looked out the window.

"That's right," said Mr. Daiches, going over to the sofa and sitting on its arm next to Nicole. He patted her on the head as if she were six years old. "This little lady wants to be a lawyer, too, Dan. I say more power to her. But first, let's get us a grandson. Right, Russ?"

Russ looked tediously at his father. "Sure, Dad," he said, walking from the window to a pitcher sitting on the hearth. "Anyone want more mulled wine?"

"Hey, listen," Evelyn called out, turning up the radio. A weather report calling for four to six inches resounded through the room. There were more words about cold northern air meeting warm southern moisture, but Dan scarcely heard them. He looked at the five people in the room with him and realized that he wanted to spend as little time as possible in their company.

"Perhaps I'd better be going," he said quickly, glancing first at one, then another of them, Nicole's gray eyes unable to affect him now. "If I leave now, I can probably get home before dark." He knew this to be untrue, but the thought of spending a night among these people seemed stressful. He stood and placed his cup on an end table.

"We wouldn't hear of it," said Mr. Daiches. "Go and call your folks. We have plenty of room. We can put you up here very comfortably until the weather improves." He pointed at the ceiling with his glass, obviously indicating rooms upstairs.

"Thank you sir. But I really should get back. My grandfather needs me." Dan edged toward the door, avoiding Nicole's eyes. "It's very kind of you. But I think..."

Then Mrs. Daiches was beside him, locking his arm in hers. "Nonsense, Daniel. Your parents–excuse me, your grandfather– wouldn't want you out on the highway in weather like this. Now come with me." She led him to a phone on a table in a corner of the room near a window.

He looked out as they passed. The snow was falling as heavily as ever, and the wind was blowing in gusts of at least twenty-five or thirty miles an hour. The only sensible choice, he realized, was to stay. Despite that, he knew that if free to choose he would take his chances in the storm. At that moment he ruefully remembered Ramona's warning. He was somewhere he shouldn't be–because of his glands.

He reluctantly picked up the receiver and dialed his grandfather's number. The phone rang only once before the Deal patriarch answered. "Grandfather," Dan began tentatively.

"Daniel. Thank god, boy. They're calling for eight to ten inches of snow here. How are you going to get home?" Grandfather snorted. Dan smiled. His grandfather always snorted when he was agitated.

"I... I'm not coming home tonight, Grandfather. I'm going to stay the night here." Dan had long known that it was best to broach bad news to his grandfather as quickly and directly as possible.

Grandfather snorted again, more vigorously than before. "Where is 'here'? That girl's house?" he asked in stern Tidewater inflections.

"Her parents' home, Grandfather." It occurred to Dan that since Mrs. Daiches was determined to have him stay that she should have the task of placating the old man. "Mrs. Daiches is right here, Grandfather. Would you like to speak to her?"

"Mrs. Who?"

"I'll put her on, sir." He handed the receiver to Mrs. Daiches. She gave him a careful look to see what his game was, then took the phone and began talking to Grandfather Deal.

Dan looked at Evelyn. She was standing by her mother, trying to piece out the conversation from only her mother's comments, smiling occasionally, giving off the apprehensive excitement of a child awaiting expected permission for some long desired enjoyment. She smiled at him, a strange smile that suddenly frightened him.

He turned his attention to Mrs. Daiches hoping for relief from the feeling of predation he sensed in Evelyn's smile.

Mrs. Daiches was dexterously handling his grandfather; she seemed capable of crooning the exact melody necessary to soothe his savage breast. Finally she turned and handed him the receiver with a smile that reminded him eerily of Evelyn's.

"Grandfather?" he said uncertainly.

"Daniel, Mrs. Daiches assures me that you'll be quite comfortable and safe. She seems a very fine woman." The old man sounded downright pleased that Dan was staying.

"Yes, Grandfather." Dan felt somehow that his grandfather had been taken in. He felt, too, that...

"Do you have money?" his grandfather asked, interrupting his ruminations.

Dan wondered why he would need money. "Yes sir."

"What will you do for clothing?"

Dan thought for a moment. "I... I have some things in the trunk of my car that I meant to get Maisie to launder. I'm sure Mrs. Daiches will allow me the use of her laundry room."

"I'm sure she will," Grandfather Deal said cheerily. Then the old man turned serious. "When will you be home?"

"As soon as the weather allows, sir," Dan said firmly.

"Good." Grandfather cleared his throat. "Well, then. Have a good visit, son. Don't take any foolish chances trying to get home before it's safe to travel. I'll look forward to your homecoming. Be careful, Daniel."

"I will be, sir. And I'll be home as soon as I can. Goodbye, sir." He hoped his farewell sounded to Evelyn and her family like familial devotion rather than distaste for his hosts. He wouldn't want to be thought impolite.

He was about to hang up when he heard Ramona's voice calling through the line. "Dan? Are you still there?"

He put the phone back to his ear. "Yes, still here."

"Wait just a moment until Grandfather goes away." Dan smiled as he imagined Ramona shooing Grandfather out of earshot. "Dan, is she close by?"

He looked at Evelyn standing just by him and smiled, insincerely, he suspected. "Yes."

"I don't like this, Dan... and neither does someone else," she said ominously.

Dan frowned. It was not like Ramona to play guessing games. "What do you mean?"

"I mean, someone has called here three times today asking for you, wanting to know if you were at Evelyn Daiches' house, *et cetera*."

"Who?" Dan asked. He couldn't imagine who might call.

Ramona's voice took on a confidential tone. "He wouldn't say at first, so I refused to answer his questions. Then he told me he was Jason Manetti. I didn't know what to do. He sounded angry that you might be there."

"I see." Dan frowned more deeply. He didn't see, really. Why would Manetti care if he were with Evelyn? Hadn't he gotten them together? It must be some game Ramona was playing with him.

"I told him you were there," she said.

"I see."

A pause. Neither spoke.

"Don't you want to know why?" Ramona asked finally.

"I suppose you told him because it would have been impolite not to after he'd identified himself," Dan said calmly.

Ramona sighed. *Men. Gentlemen. God help her.* "No," she said teasingly, "that's not why. I told him hoping he'd come there and make a scene or something and you'd have to come home."

"I see." He could feel Evelyn's eyes, all their eyes, on him. He'd been on the phone too long. Still, she had told him about Manetti. Whatever that meant.

"I don't like her, Dan." Ramona's voice was almost a hiss.

"You've never met her," he whispered hoarsely.

"I don't care. Something about your being there makes me uneasy."

Dan looked out at the falling snow. He shook his head. It was useless trying to reason with women. "What did Manetti want? Did he say?"

"Evidently, just to know if you were there. When I told him you were, he said, 'That's all I wanted to know. I gotta make another phone call. To a friend of mine in Lightfoot, Virginia.' Then he said he'd like to meet me sometime and hung up without saying goodbye."

"That sounds like Manetti." Then he added sternly, "Well, you don't need to meet him." Dan sighed. *I should never have come here.* "Well, I'll talk to him, and you, later."

"Come home soon, Dan," Ramona said suddenly. "Come home soon. Grandfather's motioning for me to get off the phone. Be careful coming home. I love you, Dan."

"Me, too. I'll be careful," Dan said breezily to allay the suspicions of Ramona who seemed to be straining to overhear while appearing not to listen. "Tell Grandfather not to worry," he added. "I can probably get back by tomorrow evening."

His peripheral vision picked up Evelyn's frown. "Bye, Cousin Ramona," he said, exaggerating his accent. Then in a whisper, "I love you, too."

"Bye, Dan."

"Bye."

He put the receiver down and turned to face the Daiches family. The two men were standing near the fireplace talking, serenely uninterested. Nicole was stretched out on her sofa contemplating her mug. Evelyn and Mrs. Daiches stood close at hand smiling, predatory.

Dan was reminded of a picture in his confirmation Bible of Daniel entering the lions' den. Like his namesake, he held out his hands palms upward, and looked toward heaven.

"What are you doing?" Evelyn asked stepping forward and taking one of his hands.

Dan shrugged and smiled and let her lead him toward the fireplace.

XIV

They had a late lunch, soup and sandwiches. The topic of conversation at the meal was college. Both Mr. and Mrs. Daiches were impressed by the fact that Dan had attended the University of Virginia. Russ reported that he and Nicole and his father had attended the University of North Carolina.

This information seemed some sort of trigger. Mr. Daiches began to recite, with Russ joining in (Nicole merely watched with a sort of feline disinterest), the following cheer/poem/pledge:

> I'm Tarheel born,
> And Tarheel bred,
> And when I die,
> I'll be Tarheel dead!

This recitation was accompanied by (on Mr. Daiches' part) appropriate gestures for infancy, maturation, and death.

After they had finished, Nicole resumed the conversation. "Does the University of Virginia require its students to learn any such performance poems, Dan?" Her husky voice oozed irony.

"I'm not aware of any," Dan replied politely. He refrained from smiling by power of concentration. He saw no need to offend his host.

Nicole sipped her soft drink and smiled sardonically. "You probably spent too much time in the university library. Not enough time enjoying college social life." Something in her tone made Dan think that she thought that perhaps Russ should have spent less time on the social, more on the academic, as she had obviously done.

Dan saw Russ look askance at her, a look that suggested that the topic of study must have indeed been a contentious one between the two during their undergraduate years. "Perhaps I did," he said lightly. "I certainly didn't meet anyone as charming as Evelyn in the U.VA. stacks."

He felt Evelyn's knee against his own under the table. He turned to her and she smiled at him, a smile of pleasure and gratitude. Dan then understood that there was some sort of bad blood between her and Nicole and that he had been her champion, even if accidentally.

Evelyn leaned over and whispered a promise of carnal delights in the coming night. Dan, to mask his embarrassment and pleasure, began to talk quietly and earnestly about a point of law.

"It's not nice to whisper at the table," Nicole purred.

"It's not nice to do any number of things at the table," Evelyn said, too loudly.

Dan turned to the others. Mr. and Mrs. Daiches stared for a moment, then returned to their soup. They were evidently used to such scenes. Russ, spoon poised between bowl and mouth, looked from Nicole to Evelyn to Dan and back again, his eyes narrowing as if he suspected something he couldn't prove. He turned back to Evelyn with a look of cool disapproval.

She felt a powerful urge to slap him. He certainly understood that Nicole was mocking her father and brother. Why was he disapproving? Then she realized it probably had something to do with his sense of decorum. He would expect her to corner Nicole somewhere and tell her off. That would be his way. Suddenly she felt a great upwelling of affection for him. He wanted things to be right, to be done right. He was what her family needed.

His face softened and he smiled. She was a woman. Useless to be angry with her. Better to correct her in a calmer moment. She was very lovely.

There was perfect silence.

Dan shifted his attention from Evelyn to her mother. "This is delicious soup, Mrs. Daiches," he said vapidly.

Mrs. Daiches smiled at him, relieved to have the tension dispelled. "It's Campbell's," she replied cheerfully.

Russ asked Nicole to pass him another sandwich and the meal continued.

XV

Evelyn helped Mrs. Daiches clear the table after lunch. Dan went out to his car to get clothes, some things he'd left in a laundry bag in the trunk. Mr. Daiches and Russ went off to shoot pool in the basement game room. Nicole simply disappeared.

As her daughter scraped remains from the plates and bowls into the garbage disposal, Mrs. Daiches asked calmly, "What were you and Nicole arguing about at the table?"

Evelyn searched her mother's face. She wondered if she knew the extent of the rivalry between herself and Nicole. "We weren't arguing, Mother. I just can't stand it when Nicole makes fun of Daddy and Russ."

Her mother nodded calmly and loaded the last of the dishes Evelyn handed her into the dishwasher. "I thought so." She closed the machine, then turned to her daughter. "Nicole's not happy," she said earnestly. "She wants more from her life than being Russ's wife and a mother."

Mrs. Daiches thought of her own life. She had given up her plans to teach to marry Ed and rear his children. If Nicole wanted more, she could not blame her. She would wish the loneliness she often felt now that the children were grown on no other woman. "She and Russ should've waited to get married," she said quietly.

Evelyn leaned back against the sink. "I've never understood what she saw in Russ." Evelyn thought back to Russ and Nicole's college days. She had been Nicole's confidant, a younger sister. It was only later, now, when *she* was in college, when *she* needed a confidant that Nicole had turned on Russ, on her parents, on *her*.

Her mother was right. Nicole was unhappy. "Nicole is really a nice person," she said aloud, realizing as she said it how trite it sounded.

Her mother picked up a dishtowel and wiped crumbs off the counter into the sink. "Even good people can do bad things when they're hurting," she said cryptically.

Surprised, Evelyn looked at her mother. She wanted to ask what her mother thought was hurting Nicole, but Dan came into the room, his bag of laundry slung over his shoulder.

He smiled modestly at the pair. "Could one of you ladies show me the way to the laundry room?" he asked.

Both Mrs. Daiches and Evelyn came forward and offered to take care of Dan's laundry.

He demurred, maintaining that he often did his own laundry in college, a small lie. He smiled, mostly to himself. Best to play the liberated man.

"I'm sorry Miranda isn't here to do those for you, Dan," Mrs. Daiches said, commiserating pointlessly.

"Ma'am?" Dan looked at her, slightly confused.

"Miranda. Our maid." Mrs. Daiches smiled.

Evelyn grimaced. Dan Deal was not the sort to be impressed by a reference to a maid. "Oh, Mother," she sighed.

"That's quite all right, Mrs. Daiches. If you'll show me the way, I'll get started." He smiled graciously at his hostess, puzzled by Evelyn's 'adolescent embarrassed by parent' attitude. Why should having a servant be shameful?

"I'll take you," Evelyn said. They went out of the kitchen by the side door, then across a hall. Evelyn opened a door and Dan followed her down some steps into the basement level of the house. Halfway down, as Dan turned back from closing the door, Evelyn kissed him. "That's for being nice to my mom."

"I didn't know I was being particularly nice," he said. "I was polite. I always am."

Evelyn smiled and gave him another quick kiss. "I'm sure you are." She turned away and they went down. At the bottom she waited for him.

"Why did you think I was 'being nice' to your mother?" he asked as he reached her.

Evelyn smiled, a little guiltily, Dan thought. "About that maid business." She pushed back her hair with her fingers.

"What about the *maid business*?" Dan asked innocently.

Evelyn twirled a strand of hair around one finger. "It was, you know, sort of laying it on thick. Like bragging." She shrugged prettily.

Dan snorted shortly, and realized in the instant that his reaction was exactly what his grandfather's would have been. "There is nothing wrong with having servants," he said benignly. "In our household, with only men, they've been a necessity."

"But most people don't have them," Evelyn offered tentatively. "Most people..."

Dan snorted again, this time making no effort to conceal his contempt. "*Most* people neither *need* nor *deserve* them," he said haughtily. He sighed and continued, more gently, "There can only be so many aristocrats in any society, Evelyn." He smiled indulgently, a line of reasoning clarifying itself for him. "Anywhere else in America, they let anyone with money call themselves aristocrats. But only in the South do we have anything approaching an aristocracy. The combination of birth, breeding, and position exist purely here."

He paused to let his idea sink in with her. She merely stared at him.

"Any aristocracy naturally assumes the existence of under classes," he continued; "therefore, wherever you have aristocrats, you have servants. To have a servant is not a dishonor, but a distinction."

Dan's face was a beacon. He had just had one of the great revelations of his life. He had consciously realized what he had always assumed: he was better than other people were.

"Well, I'd better get to my laundry," he said quietly. He stepped past Evelyn and made his way down the basement's hallway.

When he looked back, Evelyn stared after him, her mouth slightly ajar. He shivered, as if someone had walked across his grave. He wondered fleetingly if perhaps she might have found his pronouncements too much.

As Dan retreated toward the laundry room, Evelyn came to herself. She still stared after him, but she closed her mouth. Finally, she smiled a tight-lipped smile. He was undoubtedly the most pompous, superior, self-satisfied person she had ever met. He would have to be to make such preposterous claims.

Still, he was tall and rather handsome. He was polite, attentive, and generous. When they kissed, she felt warmth through her body, as when she drank whiskey. The only other man who did that to her was that delightful bastard Jason Manetti. He was certainly better than that.

She sat down on the steps to think about how she might turn him into a tolerable potential husband. She heard the washer start.

Well, he could do his own laundry. That was something of a beginning.

XVI

He was bending over the washing machine reading something when she came into the laundry room. The rumble of the washer allowed her to enter unnoticed. She took advantage of the noise to close the door quietly.

When she stepped to his side she saw that he was reading one of her mother's romance novels. She leaned close and whispered teasingly, "Is that what aristocrats read while they do laundry?"

Slightly startled, he jumped, then turned and smiled at her. "I'll read anything," he said apologetically and put the book away on the shelf from which he'd taken it. "Strange," he added softly, cryptically.

"The book?" Evelyn glanced at the cover. Another of her mother's historical romances about steely eyed, quick-tempered gentlemen and beautiful, languid ladies. Evelyn couldn't bear their silliness. Her mother read them voraciously.

"No." He smiled again. "No, the book is perfectly normal."

"Well, what, then?"

He turned and held out his arms. She stepped forward, almost unwillingly. He swept her up to him and kissed her passionately, arching her back so that she thought she must look like the heroine on the cover of the novel he'd been reading. She broke off the kiss and leaned back against the dryer laughing.

Dan stood confused for a moment. Then he stepped back. As he stood there looking at her, she noticed that his hair was mussed. She combed it with her fingertips. He gave her such a little boy look of sadness that her urge to laugh left her.

"I was only going to say," he said quietly, "that it was strange that you were able to come in here and sneak up beside me without my noticing."

She was surprised. She'd expected something romantic. He was very good at saying romantic things. "I... I wanted to surprise you." She shrugged.

"You did."

They stood and looked at each other. Dan wanted to kiss her again, but her earlier laughter made him tentative.

Evelyn wanted him to kiss her and wondered if her laughing had made him hesitant. She leaned toward him and drew his face to hers.

After a brief, tender kiss, she drew away.

Dan wondered if he'd put her off with that speech back at the stairs. He lived with the repressed but constant fear that women thought him a pompous ass. He had been thought pompous, he was pretty sure, in high school.

The pain of others' casual mockery had led him to a policy of enforced reticence during his U.VA. years. He had been well respected then. At least by his fellows and fraternity brothers. Even in college women had treated him with an amused and indulgent indifference once they had come to know him a little.

Evelyn kissed him again, more passionately this time. She shivered and pulled herself tightly against him. She snuggled her face into his sweater.

It was then that Dan realized that Evelyn still wanted him. She still wanted him, pompous ass though he might be. A restrained sigh of relief slipped from him. "I'm sorry about earlier. I have a tendency to go on." He hoped she would understand this as a sort of apology for both his posturing and for his fumbling response to what he guessed was her attempt to be alone with him.

His natural coldness had betrayed him before, altering women's opinions of him. He had been able with one comment to change a woman's opinion of him from "charmingly diffident" to "pompously asinine." Pompous. That word again. He wondered if he were becoming obsessively fearful of being thought so.

"I'm a natural romantic," he said, laying his cheek on the top of Evelyn's head. "I've found through experience, however, that women are opportunists." He hesitated, concerned with how he sounded, but she made no response. "Perhaps pragmatists would be a better description; and as a result I've been buffeted some."

She rubbed her face against his sweater front. "Bmmff," she said.

"What?" He held her away from him.

She shook her hair to get it out of her face. " 'Buffeted.' That's the word you used. 'Buffeted.' Isn't that the word?" Her auburn hair framed her face. Her violet eyes were riveting.

"Evelyn," he said hesitantly, caught up in her look, her nearness.

"Yes?" She moved toward him instinctively, sensing her power.

"Would you get angry if I fell in love with you?" In spite of himself it seemed the right question.

She smiled and put her arms around his neck. "No." She kissed him lightly. "And I promise you something." Her eyes glittered, perhaps, he thought, with tears of joy. Or of amusement, more likely.

He put his arms around her. "What?"

"I'll try not to 'buffet' you."

They laughed and kissed each other.

XVII

After they put his clothes in the dryer, Evelyn took Dan next door to the game room. Mr. Daiches and Russ were engrossed in billiards. Russ waved as they came in. "Are you two the culprits using the washer?" he asked melodramatically.

Dan admitted his guilt.

"Dan, you really shouldn't operate the washer when Dad's trying to play billiards. His nerves can't stand the noise." Russ winked broadly.

Dan acknowledged the wink with a nod. Mr. Daiches, holding a cue in one hand and a beer in the other, began to remonstrate, but Russ cut him short. "Every time he's missed a shot, Dan, he's complained about the washer's noise."

Dan nodded agreeably. He found a seat on the arm of the sofa against the far wall and watched the game's progression. At her father's prodding, Evelyn excused herself to go get more beer and snacks.

She winked at Dan as she left. Dan smiled thinly. Not one for winking, he found himself pondering life in a family where winking must be a standard form of communication.

Russ played very well. The languid grace that marks an athlete's sense of motion extended to his billiards. They were playing nine ball. Time and again Russ made skillful shots, imparting spin to the ball to move it left or right as needed. He was clearly a superior player to his father, who, inhibited by his drinking and inferior coordination, missed even simple shots.

The game moved, to Dan's surprise, at a measured pace to its logical conclusion. Then he realized that on repeatedly Russ missed shots that he could have easily made. Each time, Dan noticed, his miss set up an easy shot for his father. Dan was reminded of how he held back on the tennis court so as to let his uncles win a few games every set. A sort of respect for Russ was born.

When the game ended, Mr. Daiches offered his cue to Dan and entreated him to 'give the boy some competition.' Dan tried to demur by pleading inexperience. Russ added his voice to the entreaty and Dan accepted the inevitable.

Mr. Daiches went upstairs to find out what was keeping Evelyn. Russ racked the balls and offered to let Dan break.

"Shouldn't we shoot for it?" Dan asked.

"Oh, ho," Russ said, "So you're not the novice you claim to be." He smiled slyly.

"I'm not completely ignorant of the game," Dan admitted, shrugging.

"Well, okay, then." Russ flexed the point of his cue at Dan as if it were an epee. "As Evelyn would say, *en garde.*"

Russ shot first and left the cue ball only three or four inches from the end of the table where they stood. When Dan shot, his ball stopped over a foot away.

"Your honor, sir," Dan said, handing Russ the cue ball.

Russ broke up the racked balls and made the one and three. He also got the four and seven before missing and leaving Dan an easy shot. Dan got the nine and eleven, but then missed an easy shot at the fourteen. Russ ran off his next three balls, then missed his shot on the eight twice, allowing Dan to salvage a bit of dignity by making two more of his balls before he closed out the match.

"Another?" Russ asked, racking the balls.

"You're far too good for me, Russ," Dan said. He laid his cue stick on the table as Nicole and Evelyn came in. Mr. Daiches trailed them carrying a bag of potato chips and two six-packs of beer.

"Care for one, Dan?" he asked, holding out the carton.

Dan shook his head. "Perhaps later. I need to check on my laundry. I think the dryer has stopped." He made his way to the door.

"Oh, let these women take care of that, Dan," Mr. Daiches said, gesturing at Evelyn and Nicole with a beer carton. He turned to them "Evelyn, you and Nicole see about Dan's laundry. We men have some serious pool playing to do."

Evelyn strolled over to her father and took a beer from one of the cartons he still held. "Daddy, this is the age of women's liberation. If *you* want Dan's laundry tended, *you* go tend it." She opened her beer and took a long pull at it, then leaned against the pool table.

Mr. Daiches laughed and shook his head. "The Indians had the right idea boys," he said, winking broadly at Dan, then Russ. "Keep 'em barefoot in winter and pregnant in summer. Right?"

Dan cleared his throat. Russ made a face and returned to playing with the cue ball. There were several moments of awkward silence.

"Well, I'll be checking my clothes now," Dan said, glad to make an exit. He went to the laundry room, removed a batch of clothes from the dryer, then added a few pieces that needed to be dried separately. As he folded clothes, he heard the door close softly behind him. *Evelyn again.* He didn't turn around.

"Dan?" The velvety timbre of Nicole's voice made the hair on Dan's neck stand up.

"Yes?" His fingers fumbled at an undershirt. He managed to fold it, then in replacing it on the dryer he managed to knock it onto the floor. He knelt to pick it up. As he started to his feet, he saw that Nicole was beside him. She wore no shoes.

She fixed him in her gaze. She leaned back against the dryer and began folding a pair of his boxers. "Tell me about law school," she said invitingly.

Dan took a deep breath. He let it out firmly and broke away from her gray gaze. He began meticulously refolding his undershirt. In precise tones he gave her an account of his first semester and an estimation of what he expected in the coming spring. He was just concluding March when the door opened softly and Evelyn came in. She came up beside Nicole as he continued his account.

Suddenly Nicole stopped him by saying, "You have nice blue eyes."

He looked at Evelyn, then Nicole. He smiled pleasantly. "Thank you. They were a gift from my mother."

Evelyn picked up a stack of his things from the dryer and put them into a basket on the floor. When she turned to get the other stack, Nicole had picked them up. She stepped past Evelyn and put them into the basket, then glided from the room as quietly as she'd come in.

Dan noticed Evelyn glaring after her. "Would you like to see a picture of my mother?" he asked as a diversion.

"Who?" Evelyn growled, evidently miffed at Nicole, or him, or both.

"My mother." Dan held out his wallet.

Evelyn took it and looked at a picture of Dan and a slender blonde who looked more like his older sister standing in front of a French chateau that had chimneys sticking up everywhere. "She's beautiful, Dan," she said simply.

"Thank you."

"Do you have a picture of your father?" She handed the wallet back to him.

"Only an old one. He's been dead a long time. Since I was quite small."

"Oh, I'm sorry. You told me that and I..." Evelyn blushed slightly.

He smiled and said, "That's quite all right. I never really knew him. Here's a photo." He held out the wallet again and she looked at a faded snapshot of a tall, dark-haired man holding a blond toddler and smiling broadly.

"He was very handsome. You look more like your mother, though."

"I guess I can't go wrong. Can I?" Dan asked.

She looked up at him, slightly puzzled.

He smiled. "You've complimented both of them. It doesn't matter which of them I look like."

Evelyn took the wallet and flipped back through the pictures to the photo of Dan with his mother. "This is Chambord," she said firmly, certain she was correct.

"Why, yes it is. Very observant."

Evelyn shrugged casually. "I was there last summer."

"Student tour?" Dan stepped to her side and they both gazed at the photo.

"Um hmm." Evelyn glanced at him askance to see if he'd meant the remark in that maddeningly superior way of his. Then she remembered something. "Oh, that's right. Your mother lives in France, doesn't she? With your French stepfather." She nodded, pleased with herself for remembering.

"Tu as raison," Dan replied, nodding sagely. He spoke beautiful French almost without effort, another genetic gift from his mother, who'd easily learned the language as an adult.

"Ah, tu parles français," Evelyn said, speaking quickly. "Moi, je le parle aussi.

Je me suis spécialisé en français à Wake Forest." Her French, more schooled than Dan's, was, nonetheless, excellent also.

"Ah, oui? Ma mère et beau-père m'ont aidé avec le français quand j'étais en France."

"Tu es allés en France voir votre mère?" Evelyn glanced at him as she spoke. She smiled fleetingly, pleased to show off her expertise.

"Pas exactement," Dan continued. "Je suis allé avec un groupe d'étudiants. Alors, quand j'étais là, je suis allé visiter ma mere."

"Je vois."

Perhaps for no other reason than that they both spoke French they laughed.

Dan picked up his basket of clothes. He put them under one arm and offered the other to Evelyn. She took it and they made their way, rather awkwardly out of the laundry room and down the hall past the game room, talking softly, conspiratorially to each other in French.

Russ and Nicole came to the door of the game room as they passed. Russ shook his head and returned to shooting pool. They could feel Nicole's cool gray eyes on them as they climbed the stairs.

XVIII

Evelyn showed Dan up to the second floor and helped him to his room. They necked briefly, then Dan went back down to the game room where he passed the time before dinner in a game of billiards with Mr. Daiches while Evelyn helped her mother with dinner. Nicole had disappeared.

Dan, ever politic, purposely missed an easy shot on the fourteen ball and allowed Mr. Daiches to win the game. Russ clapped him on the back and called him a good sport. Mr. Daiches smiled broadly and protested that he had been lucky to win.

That evening Mrs. Daiches presided over (as Evelyn told Dan later) a recreation of Christmas dinner. There was most of a large ham, a nearly untouched turkey, candied yams, cranberry sauce, and all sort of vegetables and condiments meant to turn the eating experience into an orgy of self-indulgence.

After the meal everyone but Mrs. Daiches (at her insistence) retired to the den. Evelyn and Dan sat on the sofa. Nicole and Russ sat on the love seat facing them. Mr. Daiches tended the fire and soon had it blazing merrily. As the snow fell and the fire glowed, the foursome made conversation out of the air, which seemed to be the only thing they had in common.

Mrs. Daiches joined them eventually. She and Mr. Daiches sat by the bay window at the front of the house watching the snowfall. A little after ten they went up to bed.

After they had gone, Russ leaped to his feet and challenged the assembled company to a rousing game of table tennis doubles. Nicole declined offhandedly; Dan demurred graciously.

Evelyn, however, accepted her brother's challenge and the two of them went off to the game room muttering threats at each other usually reserved for heavyweight boxing opponents.

Nicole moved to the sofa next to Dan. She curled up on the sofa, knees drawn under her, head resting on her arm that was laid on the sofa's back, and watched him.

Dan leaned back and stretched out his legs. He looked from Nicole to the fire to Nicole several times. Finally, to break the silence, he said, "So. We're alone."

She didn't respond. A log slipped in the fireplace making a particularly loud crackle. Dan looked away from Nicole to see if any sparks had landed on the carpet in front of the hearth.

"I envy you," Nicole murmured.

Dan glanced back to her. "Excuse me?"

"I envy you," Nicole repeated. She raised her head and looked at him, a look like the one that had made him uneasy earlier in the day.

He sat up straight. "Why?" He asked.

She turned from him and looked into the fire.

Dan thought that perhaps he had misunderstood her. Perhaps she was talking about something else and he had mistakenly thought she was being personal. Perhaps, he thought, she was searching for something, something more than her life with Russ. The law perhaps. He realized that Ramona had warned him rightly that men always jumped to the wrong conclusions about women.

She looked back at him. "I envy you," she said huskily, with a trace of anger in her voice, Dan thought, "because you're doing something you want to do. Because you're…"

She stopped suddenly, got to her feet, and went to the fireplace. She took up the poker, so roughly that the tray of fireplace tools rattled, and punched furiously at the fire.

Uncertain how to respond, determined not to be drawn into what he saw as an imminent confession of domestic unhappiness, Dan glanced about the room, trying to think of a polite way of escaping. His eyes lit upon a bookcase on the wall opposite where he was. The books were handsome to look at, leather bound (at least it looked like leather) volumes with gilt lettering on the spines. Dan got up and went over to examine the books more closely.

He opened the glass doors of the bookcase and scanned the rows of texts. Their matching bindings made them seem at first glance all of a piece, but a closer look revealed that they were a set of some sort, rather like the Harvard Classics. There was a whole row of philosophy, another of poetry, another of novels and short fiction.

Dan let his eyes move slowly across the books, past Aristotle, past Boethius, past Locke and Kant and Schopenaur and Heidegger, then on to Bergson and Sartre. He skipped over the poetry shelf (Dan felt in a decidedly unpoetic mood) and let his hand brush across the backs of the fiction.

He started to take first *Clarissa*, then *Pride and Prejudice* from the shelf, but each time he let the book fall back into place. Finally he pulled *David Copperfield* down and thumbed through the text aimlessly, stopping at last at the ball scene where David dances with the eldest Miss Larkins.

He immediately became absorbed in reading. It was both his strength and weakness that he could ignore the outside world and immerse himself in books.

Nicole left the fireside and came over to him. When he finished the scene, he took the ribbon bookmark and saved his place. He put the book under his right arm and offered Nicole his left. "Shall we join the others in the game room?" Dan asked.

"I was going to tell you why I envied you," she said, her voice low, thrilling.

Dan, determined not to become involved in a tête à tête, replied brightly, "Yes? Well, I don't have much to envy."

"I was only going to tell you," Nicole said, her voice suddenly scornful, "that I envy you because you're so comfortable. Comfortable. That must be nice."

She withdrew her arm from him and left him standing by the bookcase. As she disappeared into the darkened hall, it occurred to Dan that he had been rude. Still he reasoned, it would have been worse to have allowed Nicole to make him privy to information unsuitable for one in his position.

Thinking about this made him wonder about his relationship to Evelyn. Ramona's warning about men and their glands echoed in his mind again. "Humph," he grunted aloud. Ramona and her pronouncements. One did one's best given the circumstances. That was the gentlemanly way. What mattered was attitude.

He made his way down the dark hallway to the door at the top of the basement stairs. His hand on the knob, he suddenly felt warm breath on his cheek, his ear. "Hello, Daniel," whispered Nicole matter-of-factly.

Dan jumped and dropped his book. As he knelt to pick it up, he heard her voice above him. "That's the way to treat a woman, Dan. Kneel at her feet. Just don't look down. Those feet might be clay."

Her laughter, low and wicked, brushed by him as she did. He saw a flash of light as the door into the kitchen opened, then she was gone.

Standing in the darkness, Dan shook his head. He clutched his book more tightly to him. She must be very unhappy, he thought. Perhaps a touch mad.

That thought frightened him. Due to his mother's experience, he had a real fear of madness. He sighed deeply to relax, assuring himself that she was only fretted with his evasion.

Dan had no understanding of practical jokes, though he had occasionally been the butt of them, especially in high school. If Nicole's practical joke had served to allay her anger with him, he was content to forget it. He shrugged and made his way down stairs, the light of the game room beckoning him.

XIX

Nicole never came down to the game room. Dan half-read David Copperfield, half-watched Russ and Evelyn play table tennis until after midnight.

One particularly fierce game drew Dan's attention entirely away from his book. Both of them were skilled players, and each knew the other's games so well that watching them play was an exercise in monitoring subtleties.

Both played with abandon. Once Russ hit a superb smash that by some miracle Evelyn managed to return. His failure to overcome her seemed to enrage Russ, and he smashed the ball back across the table again. At *her*, Dan thought. He snapped his book shut and stood, watching them, ready to defend Evelyn who had simply squatted when she realized Russ's intent. The ball sailed harmlessly onto a chair at the end of the room. Russ crossed his arms, disgusted with himself. Evelyn peeked over the edge of the table. She began to giggle. He followed suit. Soon both were lost in laughter.

Evelyn noticed Dan and pointed at him, laughing even harder. Russ looked over and laughed more uproariously than before. Dan's response was to resume his seat, reopen his book, and begin reading again. This made them even more amused.

After they had regained their composure, Evelyn came over and ruffled Dan's hair. He looked up at her ingenuously. "Yes?"

She eyed him narrowly, trying to determine if she had misapprehended his action. His face betrayed something that told her she had not. She leaned down until her forehead touched his and put her arms about his neck. "You were upset at what Russ did, weren't you?" She whispered.

"A bit," he replied reluctantly.

She smiled. "Why?" She asked coyly.

"I thought he was being abusive."

Evelyn thought he looked cute being so solemn. "And you were going to protect me weren't you?"

Dan was embarrassed by her 'cootchy-coo' tone. He hated purposeful cuteness. "I suppose."

93

Evelyn turned her cheek against his forehead. "You're a real gentleman, Dan Deal," she murmured indulgently.

Dan's heart softened at her tone. "Thank you," he said quietly. "I pride myself that I am."

Russ tapped the ping-pong table with his paddle. "Are we going to finish this game? Or are you going to coo at poor Dan all night?"

Evelyn stood up straight, her hand on Dan's shoulder. "Perhaps Dan likes to be cooed at. Besides, he would never try to kill his sister with a ping pong ball." She wrinkled her nose contemptuously at him thinking Dan would find it cute.

Dan thought about how abhorrent he found such behavior.

"Would you, Dan?" Russ asked suddenly.

"Would I what?" Dan, taken by surprise, replied. He had not been paying attention to the exchange.

"Hit your sister with a ping pong ball."

"I don't have a sister." Dan thought this answer might diplomatically excuse him.

Russ, however, was determined to get an answer. "Well, a cousin, then."

Dan thought of Ramona. He shrugged. "I'm not sure, Russ."

"Not sure?"

"Well," Dan said, "we never play table tennis." He smiled with his mouth closed.

That answer seemed to satisfy Russ, for he chuckled and went to fetch the ball.

Evelyn bent over quickly and kissed Dan on the nose. "I'll finish this game and then we'll go to bed." She winked and turned to go play.

"We?" Dan smiled, incredulous, although the prospect of committing such a sin sent a pleasant tremor through him.

Evelyn arched her eyebrows. "Wait and see," she whispered. She brushed his cheek with her fingertips and trotted to her end of the table. "Okay, Russ, I'm going to finish you off."

"She probably will, too," Russ said to Dan in an aside.

They played the rest of the game uneventfully. Russ's statement was prophetic. Leading eight to six at the time of his tantrum, he played poorly, almost too poorly, the rest of the game. Evelyn won easily.

He was a gracious loser. He came around the table and hugged Evelyn. He went to Dan, who had gotten to his feet at the game's end, and shook his hand vigorously. Dan was reminded of Lefever.

Only then did Russ remark Nicole's absence. "Where's Nicole?" he asked, glancing about the room as if she'd be in a corner like a forgotten umbrella.

"I met her at the door to the basement stairs as I was coming here, but she went into the kitchen as I came down." Dan was careful to sound offhand so as not to suggest any intimacy between him and Nicole.

"Weren't you two in the library together?" Evelyn's eyes on him were sharp. She had purposely gone off to play with Russ so that Nicole could talk to Dan about law school. She wondered why he seemed to be hiding something. *Damned men. All alike.*

"Yes, but she left while I was reading," Dan said hurriedly. He smiled, he hoped innocently, at her. He could tell she was suspicious, but he couldn't allay her suspicion without compromising Nicole to her husband. She should know that. *Women.*

"Oh, she runs off like that sometimes," Russ said, frowning. "Don't pay any attention to her." He looked thoughtful for a moment, then smiled and winked confidentially at Dan and Evelyn. "Well, I guess you two want to be alone. To *discuss* things."

Dan found his emphasis on the word *discuss* rather *rapprochement*. It put him in mind of Defoe's use of the word *conversation.*

Evelyn snaked her arm through Dan's. "Now that you mention it, Russ, you *are* in the way." She wrinkled her nose again and Dan wished he were at liberty to disentangle himself from her.

Russ waved a disparaging hand at her. "Well, good night, then." He tapped Dan's chest. "And good luck."

"Good night, Russell," Evelyn said, jerking her head toward the door.

"I'm going, I'm going," he said good-naturedly as he disappeared into the hall.

As soon as she heard him close the door at the top of the basement stairs, Evelyn drew Dan's face to hers and kissed him.

She reached under his sweater and traced her fingers down the buttons of his shirt. "Ready for bed?" she asked coyly.

Dan feigned a yawn. "Yes, actually. It's been a long day."

She took her hand from underneath his sweater and pulled him against her, her arms about his waist. "I said *bed*, not sleep."

"There's a difference?" Dan asked, coy in his turn.

"Ce n'est pas la même chose." She looked up, chin on his chest.

He looked down. Their noses touched, then their lips.

Finally, she pulled away and, leading him by the hand, started upstairs.

They reached the second floor, tiptoed down a darkened hallway, turned left, then crept down another hall. Evelyn stopped at a doorway on her right, reached into the room, and flipped the light switch on. "Here's the bathroom."

She turned off the light and moved a little further down the hall. She opened a door on her left and flooded the room with brightness. "And here's your room."

It was a tidy bedroom done in colonial furniture, a four-poster bed its centerpiece. Dan went to a bedside table and turned on a lamp, then motioned for Evelyn to turn off the overhead light. "Now. That's better," he said, surveying the room in softer illumination.

"As I mentioned this afternoon, my room's next door." She gestured with her left hand.

"Does it communicate directly with this room," Dan asked facetiously.

She went to him and kissed him on the chin. "No," she said blithely.

"Oh."

Dan's sense of disappointment surprised and pleased her. She put her arms around his neck. "It used to, but when Mom and Dad remodeled several years ago, they changed that. Russ had this room and I had the one next door. They communicated, a sort of nursery."

She turned reflective and Dan sat down on the bed to listen to her. She stroked his hair as she talked. "When we were small we used to sneak back and forth into each other's rooms and play practical jokes on each other." She looked toward the window, remembering. "I remember the Easter Sunday when I was ten.

Russ got into my room and filled my new patent leather shoes with water. I cried so much that when my parents went off to church they left me at home with our maid Etta."

She looked down at Dan, her eyes glistening. "I hadn't thought about that in years."

She went over to the closet door and opened it. "What a shame Mom and Dad had it sealed up." She turned to him. "She had to miss church, too."

"Etta?"

Evelyn nodded. They looked away from each other suddenly, she shy, he self-conscious. When they looked back at each other they smiled, rather abashed, having discovered something in each other without looking for it.

"I'll get you some pajamas," she said, so softly that she had glided from the room before Dan realized what she'd said.

He sat and considered the significance of the moment just past.

Evelyn returned. He looked up at her and she held out the pajamas. Dan studied the pajamas several moments. When he looked up at Evelyn, she was studying the pajamas, too.

Suddenly, everything–their pondering of pajamas, his being there with her, their relationship–seemed ludicrous. Dan dissolved into laughter, falling back onto the bed and taking no measures to conceal his mirth.

Evelyn stared at him, confused by his sudden change of mood. Then she thought she understood; the formality of pajamas, when they had slept together naked, probably struck him as silly. When she thought about it, it seemed silly to her, too. She giggled, tossed the pajamas onto the bad, and crawled on top of him.

Afraid he had offended her somehow, Dan tried to stifle his laughter. She giggled and kissed his face repeatedly, then licked a tear of laughter from his cheek. Her mouth found his.

When they stopped for air, Dan waggled his hand at the lamp and Evelyn reached over and turned it off.

XX

When Dan woke the next morning, he could hear the clicking of sleet on the windowpanes. He frowned. He had hoped for clearing weather and a warming trend.

He turned in the bed and looked out the window. Even in the weak light he could tell that snow was still falling along with the sleet. Sighing, he turned back to the bedside table and checked his watch. Surprisingly, it told him that it was only six-thirty. He decided to get an early shower before anyone else was up.

He sat up in the bed and felt around, trying to find the pajamas Evelyn had brought in the night before. He finally had to turn on the lamp.

They lay on the floor at the foot of the bed, unused. He smiled as he shook the pajamas out and put them on. He wondered idly when Evelyn had gone to her room.

After gathering some clean clothes from his laundry basket, he went to the bathroom. There he found laid out shaving cream, a disposable razor, a toothbrush, and a note:

I remembered you're an early riser. See you at breakfast.

Evelyn

After he'd gotten back to his room and made his bed, he looked for something to read. There were no magazines in the room, but *David Copperfield* lay on the bedside table, so he picked that up and lay across he bed on his stomach to read.

He couldn't get absorbed in it. After several minutes of half-hearted trying, he let his attention drift to the window. In the growing light he could see that the snow still came down, though not heavily as before. The sleet continued to clatter on the panes. Looking at the snow recalled to his mind another incident with Ramona:

They were sledding on the hill behind her parents' home. Dan had gotten a new Flexible Flyer sled for Christmas, and they were finally getting to use it a month later.

He'd lie on the sled at the top of the hill. Ramona would give a push to get them going, then flop onto his back and cling to his neck as they scooted down the course her father had helped them make. It was a winding track around trees and bushes and ended at the edge of a small patch of woods. Their rides together were fast, but Dan always wanted to go faster. He was eleven, Ramona, only eight.

Sometimes Dan rode down alone at the breakneck speed he liked, Ramona breathlessly watching. At other times he would urge Ramona to go down by herself. She was fearful of losing control of the sled. Dan mocked her, calling her a baby.

At last, she agreed to try. He had her lie down on the sled, even though she wanted to sit up. He gave her a ferocious push, much harder than she had given him.

She slashed down the hill, brushing the trunks of trees, barely keeping the sled on track, grazing bushes so that they threw snow on her. Just before she would have gone into the woods, she tried to stop the sled and lost control of it.

The right front corner slammed into a tree. Looking like a rag doll, Ramona flew sideways into the tree trunk. She wrapped almost completely around it, her stomach and chest mashed against the tree trunk, then tumbled onto her back and lay still, partly on, partly off, the sled.

Dan ran to her as fast as he could, twice falling on the slippery sled course. When he reached her, she was gasping as he had seen a trout do that his Uncle Charles had caught. In panic and anguish, not knowing what else to do, he began to yell at her. "Breathe, Ramona," he screamed.

Still she gasped.

"I said, *breathe!*"

She groped for air. Dan lost all self-possession. He fell to his knees, grabbed Ramona's shoulders, and began to shake her. "Breathe, damn you, breathe," he roared, tears starting. He held them back.

Her eyes widened for a moment, then she went blank. Her head slumped to one side.

He genuinely thought he had killed her. His casual cruelty and foolhardiness crushed him down with all the weight of a child's guilt. He had killed his cousin, the person he loved most, and cursed her as she died.

He got to his feet. He stood over her and looked at her body, his face expressionless. He didn't cry. It took a supreme effort, but he did not cry.

After a few long, difficult moments, he looked away into the snowy distance. He stood there letting the cold seep into him, half-wondering what death must be like. His father was dead, his grandmother, too. Now Ramona. He wondered if everyone he loved were going to die.

Perhaps death might not be so bad. It occurred to him that he had killed Ramona and that he would have to go to the electric chair for that. The thought had comfortingly tragic possibilities.

Striking a heroic pose, he looked into the snowy woods. Grandfather had just finished reading *A Tale of Two Cities* to him two evenings before. Somehow he managed to equate his murderer's role to Sidney Carton's martyrdom.

"Dan. You said a bad word."

Thus were his illusions shattered. He looked down. Ramona stared up at him. "Are you alive?" he asked stupidly.

"Yes." Painfully, she moved to a sitting position. Dan knelt and helped her. She pointed with her left hand. "The sled's broken."

He looked and saw that she was right. The right sled guide had sheared off, and the broken piece lay several feet away, sticking up out of the snow like a boundary marker. "I thought you were dead," he said, looking at the sled guide rather than at Ramona.

"What would you have done if I was?" she asked. He turned to her. Their faces were full of childish solemnity.

Dan shrugged and said casually, "Let them send me to the electric chair."

"They wouldn't do that," Ramona said firmly.

"Why not?" Dan looked at her incredulously, knowing she was going to argue again. She always argued with him. She even argued with Grandfather. Everyone in the family said that she should have been Stuart Deal's child and that Dan should have been Uncle Arthur's. Ramona had Stuart Deal's strong-willed independence of mind. Dan had his uncle's passive arrogance. As Grandfather Deal observed, Ramona had never met a soul she wouldn't argue with, and Dan had never met one he'd stoop to argue with. Except perhaps Ramona.

"I'd tell them not to." Ramona shook herself and snow flew from her like an aura.

"You couldn't do that if you were dead," Dan replied patiently.

"I'd tell them before I died."

"You were already dead."

"No, I wasn't."

"Yes, you were."

"No, I wasn't."

"Yes, you were," Dan said aloud.

"No, I wasn't," Evelyn whispered, lying down on the bed beside him; a terrycloth bath robe her only clothing. "With whom were you talking?" she asked.

"My cousin Ramona." The wind came up and began whipping snow and sleet against the window. Dan reached over and took Evelyn's hand and kissed it. Holding her hand between his two, he told her the story of the sledding accident.

"And for some reason, I said, 'Yes, you were' aloud as you came in," he concluded.

"What finally happened?"

"We kept saying 'yes' and 'no' for some time until Ramona broke into the giggles. Then I towed her home and confessed everything. At least I tried to. Ramona kept gainsaying me. Finally Aunt Edith gave up and told us that we couldn't sled anymore unless Uncle Arthur or Uncle Charles was around. Of course that rule was forgotten by the next snowfall."

Evelyn slipped her hand from between his and rolled onto her back. "Do you know what *I* think?" she asked mischievously.

Dan smiled. "About what?"

"Your little story."

"No. What do *you* think about *my* little story?" He moved to kiss her, but she held him at arm's length.

"Don't try to overwhelm me with your masculine charms. *I* think you told your aunt that you were guilty, all right. But you did so in such a way that *you* made *yourself* into a sort of martyr. Poor Ramona. *She* was completely taken in."

Her sarcasm angered Dan momentarily. It was all right to tease, but he didn't like jests that questioned his conduct.

Without warning, he lunged across her and pinned her arms to the bed. She struggled, first in play, then in earnest. Even when he knew the joke had gone too far, Dan did not free her. The feeling of power he had over her gave him a pleasure he'd never known before. He felt an erection stir, and his heart went out to her a little. She was, after all, only a woman.

Evelyn ceased struggling suddenly. She felt him stiff against her thigh and realized that he was enjoying himself. From that moment she hated him a little. He was just another man.

Closing her eyes to hide her feelings, she put on what she thought would be an air of theatrical bravado. "Do what you will, sir," she said, sounding more serious than she meant to. "You cannot change the truth."

Dan released her and lay back on the bed beside her. The look in her eyes before she closed them frightened him. He knew he'd gone too far; he wondered if he should apologize.

Then she was on top of him, and he found his own arms pinned to the bed. He struggled weakly.

"Now, villain," she said melodramatically, "admit your wrongdoing. You've been taking advantage of poor, innocent women for years. Admit it."

He burst into laughter. She hovered over him, her face seemingly stern. Each time he looked at her to speak, he laughed again. Finally, he said, nearly breathless, "I'll admit nothing. The women I've dealt with have been neither particularly *poor* nor *innocent*."

Immediately he thought that he might have made another faux pas. He stopped laughing abruptly.

She released his arms, raised herself to a kneeling position, crossed her arms, and tossed her head. "Well. You're some gentleman. To talk so about women who've given you everything, including their *honor*."

"You're wrong," he said gently, drawing one of her hands to his lips and kissing it. "I have sometimes *thought* that of women, but this is the first, and last time, I'll *say* it."

Surprised, she looked down at him. He was maddening and charming. He could never make her feel what Jason, with his rough pleasing, could make her feel. But she could never hate him as she hated Jason, either. She hated all men a little, she decided, Dan more than most, Jason most of all. Hate, love, sex, pleasure; it all seemed to work in some strange, perverse ratio.

She leaned down and kissed him lightly. "Dan?" she said shyly.

"Yes?" He stretched, satisfied that his courtliness had somehow excused his cruelty.

She said what she thought would please him. "You're a thoughtful gentleman."

"Thank you," he replied, pleased. "I try my best."

She looked coyly at him. "Your best is very nice." He was a good lover, gentle and knowing. Better than most. Not electrifying, like Jason. But pleasing. She knew better than to expect understanding. No men understood. Perhaps Alex Radford. Thinking of him, she smiled to herself. A sweet man. Just not special.

Dan smiled, too, but wanly. Her comment struck him as faint praise. "Thank you so much," he said sarcastically.

She shook her head at him, then bent down and gave him a deep kiss. He pulled her down onto him.

After a time Evelyn rested her chin on crossed hands laid on Dan's chest and asked, half-facetiously, "What about my best, Dan?"

He couldn't resist the opportunity to retaliate for what he considered her lukewarm assessment of his prowess as a lover. "Oh, you're all right, I suppose," he said, offhandedly.

She looked at him sharply, surprised at his answer. Then she wrinkled her nose. "You." Astride him, she tickled his ribs. Wiggling to escape her, he responded in kind. They were just catching their breath when Russ called down the hall that breakfast was ready.

XXI

The snow stopped abruptly just after breakfast. Russ went outside with a ruler and reported that eight inches had fallen.

They whiled away the morning with card games. A little before lunch Mrs. Daiches prevailed upon Dan to read some poetry to them Evelyn having mentioned that he read beautifully.

He was exhausted by the time he finished. Mrs. Daiches had him read, *The Lady of Shalott*; Nicole, *The Highwayman*; Evelyn, the comedienne of the group, made him read, *Casey at the Bat*. Mr. Daiches and Russ listened for a bit, but their interest waned quickly and they went to the game room to try to find a football game on television.

After lunch Dan called his grandfather and reported that he wouldn't be able to return that day. Grandfather Deal was surprisingly sanguine. His generosity of spirit was based on the solace of substitutes.

The bad weather had caused everyone–Uncle Arthur, Aunt Edith, and Uncle Charles–to stay the night at Grandfather's. Ramona planned to stay on, the old man reported.

"What about the others?" Dan asked.

"Charles hiked home to get his Jeep. He's coming back for Arthur and Edith. They want to get home and check on things." Dan heard a whispered buzz in the background. "Humph,' said Grandfather. Then more buzzing. Finally the old man sighed and said, "Ramona says to tell you she's waiting here for you."

"Yes, sir. I'll be home tomorrow, I think."

"Very good, son. That'll be fine. We'll be looking for you then."

"Yes, sir. Well, goodbye, Grandfather."

"Daniel?"

"Yes, sir?"

"Be careful, son."

"I will, sir."

"Goodbye, then," Grandfather Deal said.

"Goodbye, sir."

Dan hung up the receiver and smiled thoughtfully. It was, he knew, his grandfather's ritual to tell his loved ones to be careful. He had not done so when he'd talked to Dan's father the day of his fatal accident. From that time Grandfather Deal had instituted his ritual as a way of charming his family's lives.

When he went back to Evelyn, she suggested that they take a walk in the snow. Russ was bundling up to do some shoveling. Dan offered to help him, but Russ told him that Nicole was going with him and that there was only one shovel, anyway.

Russ then pointed out that Dan had no boots. Evelyn solved the problem by producing a pair of galoshes with metal buckles that she explained her mother had bought for her father and that he refused to wear.

Eyeing the boots, Dan concurred with his host's judgment. The galoshes were so large that even with his shoes on Dan's feet slipped around in them. They also had molded rubber bottoms that gave no traction at all.

So it was that, bundled in his pea coat, a toboggan provided by Russ, a scarf donated by Mr. Daiches, and buckled into the enormous galoshes, pant legs stuffed inside, Dan accompanied Evelyn out into the snow.

He insisted upon helping Russ for a few minutes. Evelyn disrupted his shoveling with well-aimed snowballs. When he couldn't endure her harassment any longer, he gave the shovel to Russ and chased her across the yard. She fell, and he caught her, though he fell himself as he did. He gave her a snowy face wash and she managed to put snow down his back. After a few confused moments while Evelyn patted her face to warm it and Dan danced about shaking the snow out of his shirt, they took their walk.

They made their way at first by following tracks made in the snow by cars brave enough to have ventured out at the beckoning of their drivers. At one point the track became too narrow to allow them to walk abreast. Dan stepped forward to lead the way, assuming that he should clear the path.

He reached behind him and took Evelyn's hand, but she pulled free. "What's the matter?" he asked, turning to her and stamping his feet. The galoshes were not insulated and his feet were freezing.

"Why should *you* lead?" Evelyn said, rather petulantly, Dan thought.

"I should lead because I happen to be in front," he said simply.

Evelyn's face relaxed and she started to speak, but Dan added, "Besides, it's my place to lead." Surely, he thought, she realized that he was doing the gentlemanly thing, breaking trail for her.

Her voice took on an annoying coyness. "Should I walk three steps behind you?" she asked.

Despite himself, he snickered at her. He found the situation a ridiculous one. It did not seem to him that a walk in the snow should lead to a confrontation about women's rights. He expressed himself to that effect.

"Women's rights? You think this is about *women's rights*?" Evelyn looked at him incredulously. He had behaved like a typical male. She had called him on it. That was all.

"Yes." It seemed obvious to Dan that it was.

"How childish." She tossed her head. Snow flew from the fur on the hood of her parka.

"My sentiments exactly." Dan crossed his arms. He always crossed his arms when he argued. He felt authoritative when he did so.

To Evelyn, he looked merely arrogant. "Why you smug—"

Dan didn't hear the rest because she pushed him. Hard. The snow, packed by car tires, was slick. Dan's galoshes gave him no traction. His feet flew up in the air, and, because his arms were crossed, he was unable to catch himself.

He came down hard, flat on his back. His head hit the ground and he saw stars.

At that unfortunate moment a jeep full of joy riding teenagers slid around the curve and hurtled toward Dan and Evelyn, fishtailing wildly.

Evelyn, stunned by Dan's fall and the vehicle's sudden appearance, froze. Then she fell to her knees and shook Dan. "Dan! Get up!" she cried.

Her shaking and the roar of the oncoming jeep brought Dan partially to his senses. He could tell that a truck or something was coming, and he knew he must move, that he must get out of the street. He couldn't seem to get himself going.

In desperation Evelyn threw herself on him and tried to roll him over. Dan realized what must be done and continued their rolling. Fortunately, the jeep's driver must have seen them, for it slithered its way to the other side of the street and passed by them at a relatively safe distance.

Eventually, Dan and Evelyn tumbled into a drainage ditch about eighteen inches deep, built to protect the houses on Evelyn's side of the street, some of which were built down the hill from the road bed. Dan landed on his back in the ditch, Evelyn on top of him.

Her knee crashed into his groin.

Then suddenly she was kissing him frantically and trying to talk to him between kisses. "Oh, Dan-"(Kiss) "Oh, god, I could've gotten you killed-"(Kiss) "Oh, Dan, darling, I didn't mean-"(Kiss) "Are you all right and-"(Kiss) "Please be all-"(Kiss) "Oh, Dan, say some-"(Kiss) "Oh, Dan-"(Kiss) "Oh, Dan, I love you." She collapsed on his chest, sobbing.

"It's all right," he whispered painfully. "Don't... cry. "No harm done." He reached around her and stroked the hood of her parka. The moment seemed perfect in its irony, Dan thought. The victim comforted the assailant.

Evelyn raised her head and wiped her eyes with a mittened hand. "Dan." She looked at him for several moments.

Dan attempted to speak. He desperately wanted her to move. She lay her hand on his lips and rested her head on his chest.

The throbbing in his groin lessened some and Dan became aware of the cold and wet in which he lay. He lifted Evelyn's soggy mitten from his lips. "Evelyn?"

She looked up quickly, her tear-stained face melodramatic. "What is it, Dan?" she asked breathlessly.

"Could we... get up, please?"

She looked confused by his request, so he raised his eyebrows in a mute plea.

After what seemed an age to Dan, she seemed to understand and tried to scramble to her feet. Unfortunately, her foot slipped and she was thrown back on top of Dan. She tried to break her fall by drawing up her right knee.

It came down squarely on Dan's groin. Again.

He let out a howl and jerked upward trying to get the pressure off the injured area. He succeeded in throwing her off him and out of the ditch.

She leapt to her feet indignantly as Dan fell back moaning, his hands reaching involuntarily for his groin. "What's wrong with you, Dan? Are you crazy? I was—"

Then the nature of Dan's injury became clear to her. She stopped short, knelt beside him, and gently brushed snow from his face. "I... I'm sorry, Dan," she whispered.

He managed a strained smile. She kissed his forehead. With her help Dan managed to get to his feet. Slowly, painfully, they made their way across the virgin snow of someone's yard. Dan rested his arm about her shoulders while she monologued until he felt like saying something.

"Would you like to go in?" was the first thing he said.

"If you would," she replied. "I know you must be freezing."

Dan shrugged, then winced in pain. He let out a slow breath. "No, I'm all right. The cold helps deaden the hurt, I think." He laughed and his legs went rubbery.

Evelyn caught at him and let his weight rest on her until he felt able to walk again. He stood away from her then and turned her so that they faced each other. "May I ask you something?" he said.

"Of course." Evelyn's face glowed with the cold, and Dan was once again struck by her ability to look fresh and innocent. He fought the stirrings of desire; afraid it would add to his pain.

Sensing advantage, Evelyn smiled winningly.

"Just after the accident," he began, the measured tone of his voice surprising her, "even though I was in some distress."

She smiled again, and Dan fought the urge to kiss her.

"I thought... I thought I heard you say, 'I love you.' What did you mean?"

Evelyn bit her lip. She'd overstated herself, but she didn't want to offend him with a denial, or weaken her own position with a confirmation. So she kissed him, thinking that perhaps that would satisfy him without really answering his question.

When the kiss ended, she leaned her face against his chest. "Oh, Dan," she said, half in earnest.

Dan patted her gently. He could think of nothing to say himself. He did not love her. If she loved him, he thought, it could only be the sort of love, at least in his experience that women always felt for men they slept with. Love as a convenience.

"Well. Whatever." He looked down, but she didn't look up.

Finally she stepped back and tapped him on the nose. She smiled mischievously and took his arm. They made their way silently back to her home, each trying to read the other's thoughts.

XXII

Mrs. Daiches met Evelyn and Dan at the door in something resembling a flutter for one of her sedate nature.

"We must hurry, children," she said as they stamped and brushed snow from their boots and clothing. "Aunt Jane has invited us to dinner. She wants to meet Dan."

She smiled at Dan and he felt the same uneasiness he'd felt the day before after she'd talked to his grandfather. "Jane likes a little formality, so we'll need to dress up a bit," she continued.

Dan was wondering what 'a little formality' was when Mrs. Daiches began again. "Russ and Nicole are upstairs showering and getting dressed. You two need to go right up and do the same. Separately, of course."

This last was flung over her shoulder as she went upstairs with an insouciance that Dan found out of character and unbecoming. Evelyn winked at Dan where he leaned against the wall of the foyer tugging at his galoshes. He shrugged. It was all he could think to do.

* * *

Dan was laying out a pair of khaki pants and a light blue oxford-cloth shirt when Mrs. Daiches nudged open the partly closed door of his room. "Daniel?"

"Ma'am?"

"Do you have a coat and tie with you?" She eyed the clothing on Dan's bed and, to Dan's mind, approved it.

"Excuse me?" Dan hadn't been sure about that 'little formality.' Now, he realized it meant, in a sense at least, dressing for dinner. He had to admit to himself that they were an amazing bunch.

"A coat and tie. Do you have one?" Mrs. Daiches found herself struggling to be civil. There was something in Dan's tone that conveyed not just surprise or confusion but disapproval. His distance, which she had assumed to be shyness, she now thought, might be arrogance.

At that moment she began to distrust him. He was probably sleeping with her daughter. Evelyn had had a reputation even as a high school girl. This year she had seemed to settle down some. Mrs. Daiches had hoped that Dan might be the reason.

Now, seeing his real character, even if obliquely revealed, she wished the affair between him and Evelyn over. Her son had made a bad marriage; she could not bear the thought of her daughter making one, too.

The crispness of Mrs. Daiches' tone made Dan wary. Perhaps the tone of his question had seemed supercilious. In a softened manner he said, "I don't have a coat or tie, Mrs. Daiches. I'm sorry, I didn't expect to be staying."

Leery of his charm now, Mrs. Daiches replied coolly, "Well, I'll get you something from Ed's closet. I suppose most anything will work with those." She gestured at the khaki slacks and blue shirt. "What would go with those?" she mused genially. Questions about clothes always brought out her better nature.

Dan looked at the clothes. He'd caught the change in her tone and thought it suggested conciliation. "Something in a tweed? With a striped tie, perhaps?" he ventured, taking care not to look at her.

"Yes. That would be nice," she agreed. She turned to go. "Oh," she said, turning to him and looking, for all of her, like Evelyn might in twenty years, "you can't possibly wear one of Ed's jackets, can you? It would swallow you."

She smiled. Dan smiled, too. She pondered a moment. "Well, I'll just stop by Russ's room. He probably has an extra one he could loan you."

She winked conspiratorially and left the room. Dan picked a pair of underwear from the clothesbasket and started for the bathroom.

"Dan?" Mrs. Daiches called as he came into the hall.

"Ma'am?" Dan instinctively hid his underwear behind him.

"I think the bathroom's free. You'd be well served to hop in there before Evelyn. She'll hold you up interminably. I'll put the things on your bed."

"Yes, ma'am." Dan nodded and went across the hall to the bathroom. As Mrs. Daiches disappeared around the corner, Evelyn darted from her room and crossed in front of him into the bathroom. She waggled her finger at him, inviting him in.

112

He glanced down the hall; Mrs. Daiches was nowhere in sight. He went in, closing and locking the door behind him.

Evelyn slipped out of her robe and into the shower she'd turned on. Her nudity bothered Dan for a moment; his duplicity seemed wrong. Then a literary comparison occurred that made the situation seem humorous. He realized that he was Dr. Jekyll to the mother, Mr. Hyde to the daughter.

Only later, as Evelyn lustily soaped him, did he have second thoughts about his analogy. He stepped forward into the shower spray and let the force of the water beat away his feeling of unease.

XXIII

When he got back to his room, a very nice charcoal gray tweed sport coat lay on his bed. The tie with it was a terrible purple and pink-banded thing that Dan knew he would not wear as soon as he looked at it. He donned his shirt and slacks and threw the tie over his shoulder. Then he went down to Mr. and Mrs. Daiches' room and knocked resolutely at the door.

Mr. Daiches, attired in a full-length velour robe that reminded Dan of an academic gown, answered. "Something wrong, Dan?" he asked. "Catherine's in the shower, but she told me she'd given you a coat of Russ's and one of my ties to wear."

Dan held up the tie mutely. Mr. Daiches winced, then nodded knowingly. "Catherine's old maid aunt gave me that and she hasn't been able to get me to wear it. I guess she thought she'd foist it off on you."

He ushered Dan into the room and led him to his closet on the inside wall were two large revolving tie racks. Dan turned through them quickly and found a muted red and gray rep stripe. He took it and replaced the other tie.

"Need anything else, Dan?" asked Mr. Daiches as Dan turned to go. As Dan turned to him, his eye lit on a rack of belts. He involuntarily glanced at Mr. Daiches' generous waistline.

"No thank you, sir," he said politely. "I believe I have everything I need."

"Well, I have plenty of belts and things if you need something," Mr. Daiches said, gesturing expansively at the racks of accessories.

Dan thought he sensed a desire for acceptance or appreciation. He wondered how to respond.

"They're... very nice... belts," he said haltingly. Like Daisy confronted with Gatsby's shirts, he was somehow overcome.

He turned then and made a hasty exit, calling his thanks for the tie over his shoulder. Mr. Daiches nodded benevolently with a hand gesture somewhere between a wave and a benediction.

Dan returned to his room and finished dressing, then went downstairs to wait for the others. Russ had preceded him, so they stood in the foyer and made small talk. Russ challenged him to another game of billiards. At that moment Mr. Daiches came down. He took up Russ's gauntlet. Dan retired to the den.

Alone, he scanned the bookshelves again. He had taken down Boethius' *The Consolation of Philosophy* and was reading the section 'Fortune' when Evelyn came into the room looking for him.

"Reading again?" she said teasingly. "My, you are the intellectual, aren't you?"

She posed in front of the fireplace, one hand on the mantel, the other on her hip. She wore a white lamb's wool turtleneck sweater and a wool tartan kilt of red, white, and black. She had on stylish boots.

Dan gestured at her outfit. "Are you dressed formally enough to go to your aunt's house?" He closed Boethius and replaced the book on its shelf. He walked slowly to the fireplace and took her in his arms.

"Like any man," she said, tickling the back of his neck. "The facade of civilization hiding the animal underneath."

Dan replied by kissing her. She pressed against him. He was holding her, her face against his neck, when he heard someone clear her throat.

He looked around. Nicole stood in the doorway. The lamp near her illuminated her gray eyes and dark hair. She wore black, and her hair was pulled back on one side and held by a simple comb. She was stunning.

"Good evening, Nicole," Dan said, stepping away from Evelyn. Then, almost automatically, he added, "You look lovely."

Her eyes fixed on him with a look so direct and exclusionary that Evelyn took his arm as if to physically free him from it. "Russ doesn't like this dress," she said, moving her hands down its lines, which clung to her.

Evelyn moved her arm from Dan's and faced the fireplace. "I don't like it, either," she said.

Dan turned to her and stepped close so that Nicole might not hear. "There is no need to be petulant," he said softly, disapprovingly.

Evelyn gave him a sharp glance. Dan pressed his lips together to show his displeasure. She tilted her head and said coolly, "I don't know you very well, Dan Deal."

He smiled wryly. "That depends on how you define the word 'know.'"

Evelyn studied his face for some hint as to his intent. She understood the sexual innuendo, but she couldn't fathom why he'd turned the conversation that way. *If only he weren't so intellectual. If only he was more like...* she caught herself. *Mustn't do that. Should never compare. Make the weaknesses of both too obvious.*

They were still looking intently at each other. "What were we talking about?" she asked, smiling shyly.

"About your not knowing me very well," Dan said quietly. "You made some comment to that effect."

Evelyn put out her hand and gently touched his face. "I said that?" she asked, surprised.

"Yes." Dan nodded as he spoke in a sort of double affirmation. He wondered idly if she had been considering their relationship. He didn't want her to consider too deeply until after he was gone. He hated scenes, and he felt sure that she would cause one, especially if she decided to dismiss him and he reversed the situation and dismissed her.

A woman had once dismissed him. He felt confident that he could prevent that occurring again.

Evelyn smiled at him. "I was wrong," she whispered.

Dan was trying to puzzle out both her smile and her change of heart when Mr. Daiches stepped into the den and told them that Mrs. Daiches was ready to go.

XXIV

Aunt Jane, as she insisted Dan call her, was Mrs. Daiches' sister. Her husband, who had been Mr. Daiches' roommate in college, was now senior vice-president and comptroller of the furniture company of which his friend was president.

He did not insist that Dan call him Uncle John. He preferred Mr. Murray. Dan obliged willingly.

The Murrays had one child, a daughter named Celia, who attended Duke University. Her chief preoccupation seemed to be reminding Russ and Evelyn that she attended 'the Harvard of the South.' She was a first-rate bratty snob.

"What's wrong with the University of North Carolina?" Russ waved a glass full of scotch and soda at Celia and took a seat on the sofa in the oak-paneled den. Evelyn joined him there.

Mr. Murray stood behind the bar that ran nearly ten feet down one side of the room and filled drink orders. Mr. Daiches leaned against the well-padded expanse and appreciated his drink.

Mrs. Daiches and Aunt Jane sat in overstuffed chairs across from the sofa. Celia paraded back and forth between sofa and chairs like a small child.

Dan took up a post behind the sofa to observe the action. He glanced about for Nicole and found her in a shadowy corner by the fireplace looking predatory, a glass of wine in her hand. He thought of the Rolling Stones song. 'You Can't Always Get what You Want.'

"State schools are so... *open*," Celia cooed. She smiled, superior and smug.

Dan guessed that she was a freshman.

She stepped over to the window that looked out on the Daiches' home. "Lots of lights on in your house, Aunt Catherine."

"Security," Mr. Daiches rumbled as Mr. Murray slid a fresh whiskey sour to him. Mrs. Daiches looked at him disapprovingly. He shrugged and took a long pull at his drink.

"Evelyn?" Celia said, still gazing out the window.

"Yes, Celia?" Evelyn answered, her tone sugary, mocking. She watched her cousin with a look of amused expectation.

119

"How are things at... Wake Forest?" Celia glanced over her shoulder coyly, the hesitation in her voice meant to suggest disdain, Dan thought. He decided not to tell her where he went to school, even if she asked.

"Fine," Evelyn answered, rising. She went to the bar and put down her wineglass. She went to Dan and put her arm through his. "I hope we go in to dinner soon," she whispered.

Celia left the window and came over to them. "Aren't you majoring in French, Evelyn?" she asked facetiously.

"Yes, Celia." Evelyn rolled her eyes.

"I've heard Wake Forest's French department isn't very strong." Celia tapped her cheek with a finger.

"You mean, not as strong as Duke's, don't you?" Evelyn's voice was honeyed, her delivery deadly.

"And Duke's is not as strong as North Carolina's," Dan added. Both women looked at him, Celia astonished, Evelyn surprised but pleased.

"What's that?" Celia eyed him intently.

"I mean merely that the University of North Carolina has one of the finest programs in the country for the study of French." Dan took a sip of his drink and looked placidly into Celia's stare.

"Where did *you* go to school?" Celia asked aggressively.

Dan smiled, the advantage his. "The University." He turned from her as Russ joined the group.

"The university?" Celia muttered, bewildered.

"Yes." He nodded to Celia, then drew Evelyn away. Russ began bantering with Celia about the success of North Carolina's basketball program.

"She's impossible," Evelyn said as Dan put his glass on the bar. "Ever since she started at Duke, all she does is try to make anyone who didn't or doesn't go there feel inferior. I'm beginning to hate her, I believe." She moved off toward the fireplace. Dan followed.

"It will pass." Dan held his hands out to the fire. "I saw cases of 'superioritis' with every new freshman class at the university."

"Did you have one?" Evelyn asked, her tone teasing.

"No." Dan's voice was calm, condescending. "That type tended to be those who were barely admitted to the university. I suppose each felt insecure about his right to be at U.VA., so he massaged his ego by trying to make others feel inferior."

"Well, that explains Celia. She got into Duke as a lucky alternate." She looked askance at him. "You, of course, never felt such a need," she added, her voice hinting mockery.

Dan smiled at her. "Absolutely not." He turned so that his back was to the fire. Evelyn took his arm.

"Why do you call U.VA. *the university*?" she asked.

He smiled slyly. "Call it a whim." When she frowned, he added, "It's a common nickname used among Virginians."

She shook her head. "You're as bad as Celia," she said, trying unconvincingly to sound reproving.

"Does that mean you're beginning to hate me, too?" He glanced at her, his eyes twinkling.

Aunt Jane announced dinner before Evelyn could reply.

XXV

During dinner Evelyn and Celia sat on either side of Dan. Russ had told her where Dan went to college, so Celia spent the entire meal trying to find out why he called U.VA. *the university.*

Evelyn spoke only French to Dan to aggravate Celia, who'd studied Spanish. Whenever Celia tried to say anything to her directly, Evelyn would insist that Dan translate it into French for her. She would then reply in French and Dan would have to translate that into English for Celia.

"Ladies," Dan said finally, "this grows oppressive. I suggest that if you wish to converse that you speak to each other in a mutually understood language."

At that moment Nicole, who was seated across from Dan, passed him a piece of pecan pie that had been given to her. Dan noticed that Russ gave him an odd look, so he passed the pie on to Evelyn with a gallant flourish.

Celia then passed Dan a piece of pie for which he thanked her so graciously that Evelyn pinched him on the leg. "Merci, mademoiselle," he said in response.

She looked past him at Celia who had just filled her mouth with pie. "So, Celia. Have you decided on a major yet?" she asked, then sat back smiling. Nothing embarrassed her cousin so much as having attention drawn to her eating.

Celia took some moments to respond. She swallowed her pie, laid down her fork, took a sip of water, then patted her mouth with her napkin. After that she struck a thoughtful pose, pursing her lips and pressing her fingertips together.

"What was *your* major, Dan?" she asked suddenly, tilting her head toward him.

"English," Dan said, then put a bite of pie into his mouth so that he wouldn't have to say more.

"Quite a variety of majors here," Celia said, looking about the table. "Russ in business, Nicole in political science; you, Dan, in English, and Evelyn in… in French," she finished; her hesitation with Evelyn meant to suggest gentle disparagement. "You know,

123

I'm not sure about my own major. I'm torn between dance and... marketing."

Russ guffawed. Nicole smiled contemptuously. Evelyn tried to contain her glee at Celia's revealed insipidity and got choked on her pie. She sipped water trying to regain her composure.

"Some disparity between those choices," Dan said in a cool, ironic tone. Russ guffawed harder.

Celia looked at them with a mixture of humiliation and hauteur in her face.

"Children, let's go to the den for coffee," Aunt Jane announced from the far end of the table.

Once resettled in the den, Dan noticed that Russ had become very solicitous of Nicole. Although he and Evelyn sat by her on the sofa, Russ perched on the sofa's arm next to his wife. He added brandy to her coffee at her request and complimented her outfit, freely admitting his error in criticizing it earlier. The four of them made meaningless small talk for a time, then Evelyn went over to the window. Dan followed as soon as his sense of manners allowed.

"Russ wants some tonight." Evelyn held back the lacy inner curtain and looked across her aunt's snowy lawn toward her own house.

"What?" Dan wasn't sure he'd heard right.

Evelyn looked sharply at him. "Russ wants a piece tonight. He's horny. He wants to get laid. Comprenez-vous?"

Dan shook his head wonderingly and played with a bit of food caught between his teeth with his tongue. Discussing sexual matters with women in locker room terms still scandalized him, despite an attempt to come to terms with such behavior at U.VA. He preferred the Jane Bennets of the world, the placid and compliant ones. He decided on a clinical tack. "How do you discern this?" he asked.

Evelyn smiled, self-satisfied. "Whenever Russ starts treating Nicole as if she exists, his manhood's calling for placation. He'll get it, too." She paused and looked past Dan at them. "Nicole can't seem to figure him out. Or..." She started to go on to say that perhaps Nicole had him figured him out and was only using Russ's attentions to satisfy her own needs or to give herself leverage to achieve her own ends. But she decided to keep her own counsel. Such knowledge might serve her in good stead someday.

Dan watched Russ and Nicole also. Russ had moved to the sofa beside her. They were talking quietly, earnestly, an occasional smile punctuating their conversation. Dan conceived a sudden distaste for Russ's behavior. Then he realized that it reminded him of his own manner with Alicia Pauls. The feeling was troubling. He turned from it and looked out the window.

Celia appeared in front of his face at close range. "So you're going to be a lawyer," she said.

"Yes." Her perfume was pleasant, light and alluring.

"They predict that in another ten years the profession will be glutted." She moved her shoulders and her scent reached Dan again. He did not like her, but she was a very pretty girl.

He concentrated on his answer. "I'll be established by then," he said reasonably. "And there will always be work for *good* lawyers."

"I'm sure." She wedged her way between Dan and Evelyn and looked out the window. "It's supposed to warm up tomorrow," she said, more to Evelyn than to him. "Into the low fifties, perhaps."

"I hadn't heard that," Evelyn said curtly. She reached around Celia and took Dan's arm. Celia looked at them, then stepped away from Dan, closer to the window.

"Oh, look, there's a rabbit in our yard." She pointed.

Dan leaned toward the window, away from Evelyn, scanning the dark for some sign of the rabbit. Celia tilted her head until her hair brushed his cheek. He cut his eyes at her and she smiled as she looked out the window. When he turned his head, she had moved so that their faces were only inches apart. "You should come to Durham some time," she whispered.

It was then that he felt Evelyn's fingers clutch him just below his rib cage. He glanced back at her; she was frowning.

Feeling foolish, Dan looked back out the window, aware of Celia's ruse at last. "I still don't see any rabbit," he said, trying to sound innocent.

"You know," Celia said, moving away from him. "Duke has a fine law school. Probably better than Wake's." She smiled contritely.

Dan felt her contrition was genuine, so he smiled in return.

"Dan." Evelyn spoke softly. Dan turned with some effort from Celia to her. As they looked at each other, both felt something irresistible and fateful.

Perhaps Celia felt it, too, for she left them and went to a spinet piano in a far corner of the room. She sat down and began to play Chopin's "Etude in E."

As he listened to Celia play, Dan looked at Evelyn again. He felt he wanted to know her as he had never known anyone before, in intimate, automatic ways. He pulled his eyes from her and looked out the window until the feeling passed. He felt relieved when it did.

Without looking again at her, he asked Evelyn, "Will we be here much longer?" Her reply was to lead him to the door, bidding everyone good night as she did so. Aunt Jane saw them out, getting their coats for them, checking the night sky for snow, and admonishing them to wrap up warmly. Dan thanked her for dinner and expressed the hope of seeing her again sometime.

"Oh, I'm sure we'll see more of you, Dan." She gave Evelyn a knowing smile. Evelyn returned the smile, as Dan stood by slightly nonplussed.

Then they were out in the cold.

XXVI

Evelyn and Dan went home and went to bed. Together. Without fanfare. Dan expressed qualms about parents coming in to say good night. Evelyn laughed at him.

They lay facing each other, naked, his hand massaging her thigh. Dan the lover was much the same as Dan the student: attentive, diligent, anxious to please. The main thing that had drawn him to Evelyn was her utter abandon. The first night they had made love at his house, the ferocity of her lovemaking had left him feeling almost helpless. Her ardor had not lessened. Dan was, though he tried not to admit it, awed by her.

"Remember that first night?" she whispered, moving her fingertips up his side, brushing his ribs so that he started. "Ticklish?" She smiled as he nodded at her like a small boy.

Then she drew him to her.

When Dan thought about it later, he realized that passion like Evelyn's was almost impossible to describe. At its most consuming it was like being part of an impressionist painting, Evelyn like a Degas' *la baineuse*, all thighs and breasts.

The night passed as such nights do. Dan swam in passion to rafts of sleep, each succeeding dip in the waters less a struggle, more an understanding and acceptance.

At first light he woke. He slipped from the bed, found his boxers and undershirt, and put them on. He went to the window and looked out. The sky was perhaps thirty minutes from real daylight. It was still overcast, but the clouds were moving quickly in a brisk wind. The dark shapes of trees and the dull, dark hulk of Aunt Jane's house broke the white snow and gray clouds. The floor where Dan stood was not covered by carpet, and he shifted from one foot to the other to relieve himself from the cold seeping into him.

When he looked back at the bed, Evelyn lay wantonly disarrayed, both arms flung out above her head, her breasts half exposed. Dan thought of Moll Flanders and of Tess of the d'Urbervilles. He could make no sense of how he'd connected

127

those two, so he stripped and returned to bed. He woke Evelyn, then, to paraphrase Pepys, did *tout ce qu' il a voulu.*

XXVII

Celia had been right: the weather warmed so much that, after an early morning scraping, even the Daiches' quiet street was easily passable. At breakfast Dan informed everyone that his intent was to leave right after lunch.

All demurred, Russ jovially vehement, insisting that Dan shouldn't go until he'd won at billiards. "That might mean I'd be here for years," Dan said, smiling.

Russ laughed. He seemed in an excessively good humor. "Oh, *we* wouldn't mind if you stayed on, would we, *Evelyn?*"

Her blush looked quite genuine. Dan felt if he were ruled by his heart, he might have been moved to stay another day.

Mr. and Mrs. Daiches added their own protestations to those of Russ and Evelyn.

Dan remained firm. He loaded his car with his clothes. He returned all the articles he'd borrowed: sport coat, tie, galoshes, and pajamas, to Mr. Daiches and Russ. Mrs. Daiches gave him a sack of sandwiches and a small thermos of coffee for his drive home.

"Now you'll have to return, Dan," she said as she handed them to him. "You'll have to bring my thermos back."

He smiled and thanked her.

Before he left, he called home. Ramona answered. "How's the weather there?" he asked.

"Warming up. The streets are clearing. Hint, hint."

"I'm just ready to start for home," Dan replied. "I should be there by dark."

"Drive carefully, Dan, but come home soon. It's supposed to turn very cold later tonight: an Arctic cold front or something. The roads may get icy again." She sighed. "I'm waiting for you, Dan. Here's Grandfather."

"Daniel?" Grandfather Deal shouted into the receiver as if that were necessary to reach across the distance.

"Sir?"

"Do I understand correctly that you're coming home?"

"Yes sir."

129

"Be careful, son. We're waiting for you anxiously." Dan could tell from the tone of the latter statement that it had been made to tease Ramona.

"I'll be careful. I told Ramona I'd be home about five."

"Very good. Well, be careful, Daniel."

"I will, sir."

"Here's Ramona again."

"Dan?"

"Yes?"

"I... We love you. Hurry home."

"All right. See you tonight."

"Dan?"

"I love you both, Ramona."

"Bye, Dan." Her voice betrayed Ramona's pleasure at his statement of affection.

"Goodbye. As Dan hung up the phone, he noticed Evelyn eyeing him narrowly.

"You and your cousin... Ramona, seem very close," she said, affecting idle curiosity.

"We're a close family," Dan said flatly. He wanted no coy scenes now. He took her arm and began guiding them out of the den and toward the front door.

"Do you have a picture of her?" Evelyn asked gently, stopping their progress.

Dan sighed, displeased, and nodded shortly. He took out his wallet and flipped to a picture of Ramona from her senior year in high school. "Oh," said Evelyn, catching her breath sharply. "She's beautiful."

"Yes, she is," Dan affirmed in a soft matter-of-fact voice. "This photo doesn't do her justice."

Evelyn took his wallet, studied the picture for several moments, then returned the wallet to him humbly. She felt a pang and wondered if it were love. She knew she was pretty, but this Ramona was impossibly so. Was she really his cousin? Was he lying to her? "Your... cousin, is very fond of you, I guess?"

"Yes." Dan felt the conversation beginning to circle. To try to prevent its becoming a vortex, he added, "We've always been like brother and sister: devoted to each other." His face colored as he finished. Dan, once he'd said it, found himself wondering what he'd meant.

Evelyn saw his face redden and looked at the carpet. Was his blush because his expression of family affection embarrassed him? Or was he lying about that gorgeous *cousin*? Why did she care?

She looked up at him and smiled brightly. "Tell Ramona hello for me," she said rather coyly.

Dan smiled, thankful to her for ignoring his confusion. "I will," he said warmly.

There was nothing left but to say goodbye to one and all.

Mr. and Mrs. Daiches were waiting by the door. Very cordial thanks on his part for their generous, truly Southern hospitality. Very cordial appreciation on their part of his willingness to partake of same and of their desire to offer it again in near future. Handshakes for Mr. Daiches and Russ, a kiss on the cheek for Mrs. Daiches. Then to his car, Evelyn on his arm.

"What became of Nicole?" Dan asked as they negotiated the drive. Only then did he remember that he hadn't seen her since breakfast.

"Oh, she's upstairs in bed," Evelyn said off-handedly.

"Is she ill? She and Russ disappeared right after breakfast."

"No." Evelyn smiled facetiously. "Nicole's busy."

"Busy?"

"Evelyn pulled him against her. "She and Russ went upstairs for a quickie after breakfast. Nicole's lying in bed with her rump propped up, holding Russ's semen in her, trying to get pregnant."

There was nothing to say in reply to such a revelation. Dan pursed his lips and nodded. "Well. Send her my best wishes," he said finally.

Evelyn laughed. "She'll be glad to have them, I'm sure." Then she went serious. "When will I see you again?"

"Oh, I don't know," Dan said lightly, turning and opening his car door. "When does spring semester begin?"

She pulled him around to face her. "Not until then?" she asked, surprised.

"Probably not." He shrugged and her face fell. "Unless," he continued, "you come up for New Year's Eve."

"That's Monday," she whispered, then gasped, the force of Dan's jest catching her.

He nodded. She threw her arms around his neck and kissed him ferociously.

When she let him go at last, she was off like a rocket. "I've got a million things to do before then. Have a safe drive home, Dan. I... I love you." She dashed away toward the house before he could decide whether or not to return the sentiment.

XXVIII

As he drove home, Dan reflected on the adventure just past. Like most English majors, he was occasionally prone to see his life paralleled in literature. He drove along, considering his situation, unable to decide whether he was more like Fitzwilliam Darcy in *Pride and Prejudice* or Ned Hazard in *Swallow Barn*.

The roads were quite clear and Dan made excellent time. Then, about five miles north of Danville, he had a flat tire. It took him nearly two hours to get the tire fixed (he had removed his spare the week before to transport some Christmas presents and had carelessly forgotten to replace it). They were still celebrating the holidays in Lima, Virginia, and he had a terrible time finding someone who'd come out.

So it was after seven when he turned onto the street where he lived. The house sat on a street with others of its kind: well kept Victorian monstrosities lucky enough to have escaped urban blight, just then beginning to be taken over by young professionals fascinated by home architecture.

Dan's home stood two and one-half stories high and had twelve rooms. Maisie, the long time housekeeper and only other resident of the place, went into some of the rooms only a few times each year.

The house had a mock tower, as do many such structures. Dan had appropriated it as his own while quite young. The inside of the room was octagonal in shape, so furniture didn't fit. Dan kept most of his things in a closet and a large oak wardrobe across the hall.

Despite the inconvenience of the room, it was quite romantic and appealed to that side of Dan's nature which he'd inherited from his mother and which he kept hidden from the outside world.

Dan parked behind the house and went in the back door. Maisie was in the kitchen putting away the last of the supper dishes. She closed the dishwasher as he entered and greeted him. "Well, Mr. Daniel. Glad to see you home safe. Folks here have been worried about you."

Dan smiled. Maisie always said things with a sincerity that gave whatever she said real significance.

Maisie had been with the Deal family for thirty-eight years. Dan's grandmother had brought her into the Deal home after the rector of St. Stephen's Episcopal Church asked for someone to take her in who could protect her from her husband, a saw operator at one of the Deal lumber mills, who drank and beat her.

Maisie had arrived, ostensibly as a maid, but had become housekeeper as Grandmother Deal's health failed. When the matriarch died shortly before Dan's third birthday, Maisie had become the mainstay of domesticity, a position she still held. She doted upon grandfather and grandson. They considered her essential to the household.

"Would you like something to eat, Dan?" Maisie opened the refrigerator and began taking out leftovers.

"Could I have a couple of sandwiches and a glass of milk, Maisie? I'm starved. I'll come back to eat in a few minutes. I need to let Grandfather know I'm home."

She patted his arm in her favorite gesture of affection. "Your grandfather will be glad to know you're home. I'll put your sandwiches on the sideboard," she said, then turned to the breadbox.

"Thank you, ma'am," Dan said and started out of the kitchen.

"You're welcome, sir."

Dan looked back and they smiled at each other. When he was five, Maisie had roundly scolded him for failing to say 'ma'am' and 'sir' to the rector and his wife during a visit. The scolding had impressed Dan so much that he made a habit of saying 'ma'am' and 'sir' to everyone, even to children.

Dan made his way to his grandfather's study. He found Grandfather Deal sitting in his big leather chair by the window. Ramona was at the piano. She played Debussy's *Reverie* rather tentatively.

Dan waited until she finished. "Well, I'm home," he said. They both looked up. Grandfather closed the book he had been nodding over. He picked up his cane and slowly rose from his chair. Dan met him before he had taken two steps. Their cordial handshake turned into an awkward embrace.

"I'm glad you're home safely, son," Grandfather said softly. He then added heartily, "This place seems empty without you. Ramona thinks so, too. Don't you, dear?"

His cousin had not moved from her place at the piano. Dan helped his grandfather back into his chair, then went and joined Ramona. She began to play again, a little dance by Mozart. Grandfather took up his book again.

Once the old man seemed to be reading, Ramona whispered to Dan. "You're back. Good. It's been busy around here. Phone calls and letters pouring in."

She nodded at the music before her and Dan turned the page. "I'm very popular, then," he said off-handedly.

"Quite. Although I must say, I think some of the autographed pictures of you I've been sending out might be going on dart boards rather than bedside tables."

"Manetti? Again?"

She nodded, her eyes fixed on the music, and Dan reached for the page to turn it, but she shook her head. He looked questioningly at her and she shrugged in an irritated way. "He's called three times. And a letter arrived today. Oh, and Alex Radford called. He wanted you to come to Williamsburg, but I coaxed him here, instead." She smiled at the music, confident in her charm.

"When's Alex coming?" Dan asked. Ramona glanced at him; the sharpness of his tone surprised her.

Dan recollected himself and whispered, "I'm sorry." He wondered if Alex's visit would coincide with Evelyn's. Then he wondered why that mattered.

"Some time New Year's afternoon. He has big plans for New Year's Eve, he said, and probably wouldn't be fit to travel before noon."

"Hmm." Dan pondered the piano keys, debating the judiciousness of telling Ramona about Evelyn's impending visit at once or waiting for a more auspicious moment. He decided upon another tactic.

"Grandfather," he said as Ramona flipped through her music looking for something else to play, "I've invited Evelyn Daiches to come up New Year's Eve and spend a couple of days with us. Is that acceptable to you?"

Grandfather laid his book flat in his lap and looked at Dan over his reading glasses. "This is the young woman you've just visited with?"

"Yes, sir." Dan sensed disapproval, so he added, "You spoke with her mother."

Grandfather nodded. "Of course. Charming woman. I'll look forward to meeting the young lady. Is she anything like her mother?" The old man's voice was hopeful.

Dan considered the pair for a moment. Both certainly knew how to handle men. "Very like," he said aloud.

Ramona patted his leg lightly. "Why don't you play something for Grandfather and me?" Dan asked.

She pinched his leg and he winced; then she calmly commenced the *Etude in 'E'* by Chopin.

"I heard this the other night," he whispered.

"Oh. Did Evelyn play it for you?" Ramona smiled syrupy.

"No. Her cousin did." Dan smirked.

"What's her name? Delilah?"

"No. Celia."

"Is she pretty?"

"Celia? Or Evelyn?"

Ramona glanced at him, her look critical. "Does it matter?"

"No. Actually, both are quite lovely," he replied calmly.

She missed a note and banged the piano. "Damn."

"Ramona," Grandfather said calmly without looking up from his book.

"I'm sorry, Grandfather." She began to play again, concentrating intently on the music.

"Why don't you come to my room later and we'll have a long talk about this," Dan said gently.

She didn't respond immediately, and Dan thought she had decided to ignore him. He turned to get up from the piano bench. "What's there to talk about?" she said evenly.

"Well," Dan turned back and looked at the side of her face as she played, "I'd like to know what Manetti said, and I'm sure you'd like to know all that went on at Evelyn's."

She tossed her head and leaned close as if trying to make out the passage she played. "I'm not so interested as you might think," she murmured.

"Suit yourself." Dan got up from the bench and went over to his grandfather. "Sir, I'm going to the kitchen and have a sandwich. I didn't have any supper."

"Don't you want Maisie to fix something hot for you?" Grandfather Deal looked up at him. His hair shone silver in the lamplight.

Dan studied his grandfather's graceful bearing of the weight of his years. He wondered if he would be as noble looking in his time. Dan considered that, although slowed by rheumatism, his grandfather still made his way up to his second floor bedroom each night. When his sons had offered to buy him an electric seat to carry him up and down stairs, he'd refused, saying that when he got too old to climb the stairs, it was time to carry him up to his room to die. Dan admired that proud imperiousness enormously.

"A sandwich will be fine, sir," he said, patting the old man's shoulder.

Grandfather Deal looked up again. "All right, then." After a short pause he added, "You should watch what you eat, Daniel."

"Yes, sir." Dan nodded solemnly, then turned and started for the kitchen. Ramona began to play *Fur Elise*, a favorite of his and his grandfather's.

"*Fur Elise*. That's a lovely piece," said the old man.

"Oh, no," said Ramona, talking above the sound of her playing, "this isn't *Fur Elise*."

"But I'm sure..."

"No, Grandfather. This isn't *Fur Elise*. This is *Fur Evelyn*."

Dan tried to catch her eye, but she concentrated on the piano. He left her to her playing and went to eat his sandwich.

XXIX

Ramona went to Dan's room just before midnight. Grandfather Deal had gone up to his room, as was his habit, at nine-thirty. Ramona and Dan had stayed up until after eleven without speaking to each other. Dan was disappointed because he'd hoped they might talk about his experience at Evelyn's. He wanted another view of the situation, even one of jaundiced subjectivity as he was sure Ramona's would be.

There was much to talk about. Manetti's letter alone was worth an entire discussion:

2601 Briar Lane
Winston-Salem, NC 27109
December 26, 197-

DEAL, YOU PEDANTIC BASTARD,

You won't get away with this. At Carolina I learned a term for guys like you: snakes. You may think you've 'snaked me out,' but nobody ever does that. I'll get her back.

And don't think *you'll* get off easy. Nobody gets off easy with me. I'll have my revenge on you, you son-of-a-bitch woman stealing bastard. You can bet on that, asshole.

Yours truly,
Jason Manetti

It was a singularly confusing letter. Dan had no idea why Manetti, who had, after all, arranged his date with Evelyn, would suddenly become enraged at his continuing to see her. Surely, he thought, not even Manetti would hand out a woman, especially one he had feelings for, like a party favor to be enjoyed by anyone who struck his fancy.

One thing Dan could say for certain about Manetti's letter. It was direct. If he'd had any illusions about his neighbor's character, he had none now.

As for concerns or fears, Dan felt none. He'd found blusterers like Manetti impotent when it came to carrying out their threats.

It was not unusual for Ramona to go to Dan's room on nights when she stayed at Grandfather Deal's. When she and Dan were small, she would slip into his room and crawl into bed where they would whisper until both fell asleep. As they grew older and more self conscious about their behavior, they would sit on the oval rug at the foot of Dan's bed, a quilt around them, and look out the windows into the night sky at the stars or the rain or the snow.

On this night Dan positioned the floor lamp by his bed so that Ramona could read Manetti's letter. She was lying on her stomach beside him. She wore an overlarge William and Mary football jersey and nothing else. Her ankles were crossed, and she held her feet in the air swinging them gently.

"Interesting," she said as she handed the letter back to him. He folded it and dropped it onto the floor by the bed.

"I agree. I must say, however, that I am surprised he wrote a letter. People of his sort usually just continue to phone. It says something about him, I suppose."

"Well, he's right about one thing." She looked at him archly. "You are a pedantic bastard."

"I'm surprised he, or you, know the meaning of that word." Dan smiled thinly.

In response to his sarcasm, she reached over and traced her fingers up his leg and across his abdomen. She slipped her fingers under his sweater and undid a button on his shirt. "Dan. You're wearing an undershirt. Like an old man." She patted his chest with her fingertips.

"Grandfather caught me going without one on a winter's day about fifteen years ago. He checked me sporadically for the next two or three years. By then the habit of wearing them had become engrained. You know that."

She smiled. "So I do." She tugged at his undershirt to raise it.

"By way of offering some mental diversion as you prepare to expose my body, may I ask how you keep from freezing in that outfit you're wearing? This room is not over warm." Dan looked at the three large casement windows along the outside wall. They made the tower a horror to heat, and Grandfather Deal had, on a number of occasions, tried to convince Dan to give up the room.

Dan's response, that castle towers were always hard to heat, seemed to please the old man.

"I'm hot blooded. Don't you remember?" Ramona's fingers found skin and Dan jumped. "Is my hand cold?" she asked gently, laying it flat on his stomach.

"That's part of it," he replied, slightly breathless.

She leaned over and purposely rested her breasts in the space between his arm and chest. "What's the rest of it?" she whispered, her face hovering just above his, her perfume heavenly.

Her maneuvering was all too familiar to Dan. He wanted her advice on his involvement with Evelyn, and her opinion of the situation with Manetti. "I really want to talk, Ramona," he said quietly.

She rolled away from him and lay on her back staring at the ceiling. "What do you want to talk about? Evelyn?" Her voice, though quiet, shrilled with sarcasm.

"Petulance doesn't suit you, Ramona," Dan said wearily. "Let's talk about something else. Any reaction to Manetti's letter besides *interesting*?"

She turned her face to him. She was especially lovely in the soft glow of the bedside lamp, he thought.

"Isn't talking about the letter talking about Evelyn?" she asked.

Dan smiled, conceding her point. "Yes, I suppose it is." He turned on his side facing her and propped his head on his hand. "But may we talk about it anyway?"

She tapped the end of his nose with her fingertip. "Yes." She sighed. "We'll talk about it. We'll talk about anything or anyone, including the almighty Evelyn. But then..." She stopped.

"But then?"

"But then... then it's my turn." She looked back at the ceiling and crossed her arms.

"Your turn? For what?" Dan asked.

"For... whatever." She turned to him and nodded decisively. Dan thought she looked very young.

"Good," he said aloud. "Now, about Manetti's letter."

Ramona broke in then and went on to say that Manetti's letter struck her as immature, crude, and vain, but that the writer was, as Dan himself had suggested, someone to be reckoned with.

Dan noticed that in her discourse Ramona never mentioned Manetti by name, only as 'he' or 'him.' That struck him as somehow significant.

"I wouldn't have reached that conclusion about Manetti." Dan wrinkled his features derisively.

"Your glands are doing your thinking." Ramona pulled the edge of the comforter up and arranged it over her legs.

Dan was annoyed that Ramona continued to insist that his behavior toward Evelyn was motivated by lust. "You've made that observation before," he observed dryly.

"Look, Dan," she replied. "This whole thing is based on sex. The first night you met this girl, you slept with her. I'm not criticizing that; I understand how it happens."

Dan tried to catch her eye, but she continued to study the ceiling.

"I'm willing to bet," she continued, "that when you visited her home that you had the room right next to hers. Hell, there might even have been a door communicating between the two rooms." She paused, considering the unlikelihood of her last suggestion. "If houses had such. Like hotels," she added as an afterthought.

Dan was startled by her intuition. "Actually, the communicating door was sealed up. She had to go out into the hall." Aware then that he'd over spoken himself, he fell silent.

"You've told me that much, you may as well tell me the rest." She flipped back the comforter and got up, exposing herself as she did.

Dan looked away. Ramona was his cousin; his beautiful, irrepressible, irresistible cousin.

Ramona turned down the bedclothes and got into bed. Once settled, she turned to Dan expectantly. He didn't speak.

"I was freezing, Dan," she said calmly. "If I'm going to have to listen to this rot, at least I ought to get to be warm." She snuggled farther down under the covers and, wrinkling her nose, smiled at him.

Dan got up from the bed and went down the hall to the bathroom. When he came back, he stopped by the bedroom across the hall and got a pair of pajamas and a robe. He went back to his room and stood by the bed on the side opposite Ramona.

"Great," she said. "A tall tale and a floor show, too. It's like watching a TV talk show."

Dan snapped off the bedside lamp.

"Why'd you do that?" she asked. "I can't see."

"I'm trying to prevent *your* glands from doing your thinking." He changed quickly into his pajamas and robe and got into bed beside her.

She slid close to him. "Your feet are cold."

"We're going to talk, Ramona. That's all." He moved her hand from his thigh.

"She slid violently away. "Fine. Talk away," she muttered sarcastically.

Talk away he did. He covered everything: his affair with Evelyn, Mr. Daiches' drinking, Mrs. Daiches' manipulation of Grandfather Deal, Russ and Nicole's relationship, Nicole's strange behavior with him, billiards, Aunt Jane, Celia, even Nicole's failure to see him off and the reason for that.

Mostly, though, he talked of Evelyn, especially of his understanding of her behavior and what he saw as her aim, which seemed to him to be to fall in love with him, certainly nothing to be reproached for.

When he finally finished talking, he glanced at the luminous dial of the alarm clock on his desk. It was after two A.M.

Ramona said little during his recitation, asking the occasional question or reacting to some unusual aspect of his relation tersely. During the last thirty minutes of his recital she was silent. Dan thought that perhaps she'd fallen asleep.

"Ramona?" he said softly.

"Yes?" Like the darkness, her voice was cool and quiet.

"I thought you had gone to sleep." He shrugged under the covers.

"No."

"You didn't make any comment for the longest while." He twisted around onto his side facing her. He laid his hand on her stomach. The football jersey felt thick, yet satiny, to his touch. A tingle ran up his arm and into his body.

"Dan, did I tell you what he said once when he called?" Ramona's voice in the darkness broke the spell he'd been putting himself under. He drew his hand away and rested it on the bed between them.

"I'm not sure. Why don't you tell me now, even if you've told me before?" His own voice sounded hollow and distant to

143

him, even in the closeness of the dark. For some reason, he felt he didn't want to hear what she was going to say.

"He said that Evelyn called you because he'd been calling her, trying to get her to come to Winston-Salem and shack up with him." She rolled over suddenly and threw her left leg over both of his. "Dan, forget her. Be wicked with me." She turned him onto his back and got herself on top of him, kissing him from the tip of his chin down across his Adam's apple; all the while she fumbled at the buttons on his pajama top.

Her reporting of Manetti's call and the explanation it offered for Evelyn's call to him unnerved Dan a little. It was like an unexpected loud noise in a quiet place or a bright flash of light in calm darkness.

Could Evelyn have fallen in love with him after one night? One part of him said *yes*. But another part argued persuasively that circumstances were against him. He felt uneasy.

Dealing with Ramona's advances soon drove any real thoughts about the situation from his head. Say this for Dan. He never forgot that Ramona was his cousin. He never forgot that he was a gentleman.

XXX

The back porch of Dan's home had been enclosed with thermal paned glass while he was in junior high. Some of his favorite memories of that spot were from early childhood, during the first years of his life with Grandfather Deal. Dan and the old man would sit on that open porch on summer evenings, the shade of large oak trees older than his grandfather protecting them from the afternoon sun. A gentle breeze always seemed to come up as the sun went down.

As they sat together, Dan's grandfather would tell him stories of his great-great grandfather. Augustus Stuart Deal, for whom Grandfather Deal was named, rode with his cousin, General J.E.B. Stuart, during the War Between the States. He lost a leg just below the knee in the same battle in which the Confederacy lost Stonewall Jackson. General Robert E. Lee himself came to visit Major Deal at the family plantation east of Roanoke. Great Grandfather Deal, only four at the time, sat on the great man's lap.

Sometimes, as it got dark and the storytelling lagged, Maisie would bring sandwiches and a pitcher of buttermilk. Grandfather ate tomato sandwiches, heavily peppered. Dan ate mayonnaise sandwiches, sometimes so many that Maisie and Grandfather had to go to him in the night and give him strong black coffee to settle his stomach.

The sun shone brightly as Dan came downstairs dressed for jogging. The weather was uncooperative. It had turned bitterly cold over night. The thermometer in the kitchen window showed ten degrees. Dan decided that jumping rope on the enclosed back porch would have to serve as his exercise.

Midway through his fifteen-minute workout Maisie came out. Dan walked up and down to keep himself warmed up as she talked to him. "I've fixed some country ham, Daniel. How about two or three fried eggs, some grits, and some red eye gravy and hot biscuits to go with that?"

Dan tossed his jump rope onto a wicker chair and began touching his toes. "Maisie, that stuff is terrible for us. And you know Grandfather shouldn't have that salty ham with his blood pressure the way it is."

Her face fell. Dan stopped his exercising and went to her. With his arm about her shoulders he said, "I'd love some just the same. And you know how Ramona will gobble up country ham."

"Gobble up what?" asked Ramona, as she came out onto the porch. She went to Maisie and gave her a kiss on the cheek, then made a face at Dan. "I don't gobble," she said. "Turkeys gobble."

Dan picked up his jump rope. "I rest my case," he said, smiling. "Get some exercise," he added, tossing her the rope.

Ramona tossed the rope back at him. "I prefer my own exercises, thank you." She took a portable cassette player from a bag on her shoulder and snapped it on. Tossing her bag onto the wicker love seat, she began a sort of rhythmic movement to the music.

Dan shook his head at her and went inside, leaving Maisie watching, enthralled, Ramona's svelte calisthenics. He went to the study, where he knew he'd find his grandfather sitting in his favorite chair reading his Bible. Dan went up behind him and looked over his shoulder.

Grandfather Deal was reading in First John. He looked up from his reading but stared across the room rather than look up at Dan. Listen to this, Daniel," he said.

He read, "First John, chapter two, verses 15-17: 'Love not the world, neither the things that are in the world. If any man loves the world, the love of the Father is not in him. For all that is in the world, the lust of the flesh,' " emphasizing, *lust of the flesh* and *the lust of the eyes*, and *the pride of life*. " 'Is not of the Father, but of the world. And the world passeth away, and the lust thereof; but he that doeth the will of God abideth forever.' "

The old man looked up, this time at Dan, who had taken a seat on the arm of the chair. "What is your relationship to this girl Evelyn, Daniel?"

Grandfather was stern; so stern that Dan was taken aback. His grandfather had read the Bible to him when, as a child, Dan had done serious wrong. Maisie said that it was the Baptist in him that even Grandmother Deal's converting him to Episcopalianism had not effaced.

"Well, Grandfather," Dan said uncomfortably, "she's special to me; special enough so that I've invited her here for this weekend. So that you can meet her." He moved from the chair's arm to a seat on the ottoman at his grandfather's feet.

The old man looked at his grandson gravely, then turned pages in his Bible. "James 1:8: 'A double minded man is unstable in all his ways.' " He flipped more pages. "Ephesians 5:3: 'But fornication and all uncleanness, or covetousness, let it not be once named among you, as becometh saints.' " More pages turned. "Galatians 6:8: 'For he that soweth to his flesh shall of the flesh reap corruption...' "

He looked at Dan and, leaning across his Bible, asked, "What is your relationship to Alicia Pauls, son?"

Ramona. No one else had an inkling. "We're close friends, sir." Dan felt the answer wouldn't satisfy his grandfather, but he didn't intend to say anything more until he knew the lay of the land.

"Is she your mistress?" asked Grandfather Deal. The land ahead looked rugged. Dan decided not to equivocate.

"Yes, sir. After a manner of speaking, I guess she is."

Grandfather sat up with a start. Dan's matter-of-fact tone surprised him. He laid both hands, palms down, on the pages of his Bible. "This other girl, this."

"Evelyn?"

"Evelyn. Is she your mistress, too?" He looked keenly at Dan.

"No, sir."

The old man's face relaxed a little.

"She's what I would call... a lover," Dan added with an unconscious shrug.

"Oh. You differentiate, do you?" His grandfather's tone was a sarcastic imitation of Dan's matter-of-factness.

"Yes, sir. I guess I do." His grandfather was making Dan confront his feelings for the two women. Dan didn't like it.

"Are you going to keep Alicia Pauls as your... mistress?" Grandfather wrinkled his eyes as he used the term.

"No, sir. Not now." Dan looked as serious as he could, although the urge to laugh pressed hard upon him.

"What are you going to do, then?" Grandfather Deal asked. A note of triumph entered his voice. It grated on Dan's consciousness. Self-righteousness had always been his grandfather's one serious character flaw.

Dan reached over and took the Bible. He flipped through its pages. "Matthew 7:1: 'Judge not, lest ye be judged,'" he read. Dan closed the book and handed it back to his grandfather.

The old man laid the Bible across his lap and studied his grandson's face, looking, perhaps, for some small vestige of that great sense of honor which he felt and which he wore proudly, like an epaulet on a Confederate uniform. Although he longed to, he could not see it.

Dan realized that his grandfather was in some sense gauging him; he felt, too, that he was found wanting.

Grandfather Deal arose. "You are a man, now," he said solemnly. "You have your own ways." He laid the Bible on the arm of his chair and left the room.

Dan wanted to call after him. Ordinarily his grandfather would have given him a stern lecture about morals and manners. This was an important moment, one that his uncles had told him to expect. His grandfather would now deal with him as a man.

He could not, however, help feeling troubled that the moment had come when it had.

XXXI

Later that same morning Alex called to say that he would be coming on December thirty-first rather than on January first.

"Your party fell through?" Dan asked.

"Not really. I just decided that my health would be better served of I spent New Year's Eve in quieter surroundings."

Dan thought he noted an air of resignation in Alex's voice. "Sorry, Alex," he said lightly. "I guess I'm too decorous to be a debauchee. We'll have a quiet evening out–with some good wine– and let that be the extent of our revelry."

"Perhaps a toast at midnight?" Alex asked, his voice hope filled.

"Of course. It wouldn't be New Year's otherwise. Why don't you bring some champagne?"

"How many bottles?"

The ingenuous sincerity of Alex's tone made Dan smile. "One, Alex. We'll have a toast, not a revel."

"Pity." Alex's tone was again resigned. "Well, Daniel, how about some good news? Will I get to see that gorgeous cousin of yours with whom I spoke on the phone... Ramona?"

Dan smiled again. "Surely. If she has no other plans, you may be her escort for the evening. I'll arrange it."

Alex laughed, the good-natured laugh of a good-hearted soul. Mercutio's laugh. "Make sure she has no other plans, Dan."

"I don't foresee a problem," Dan replied calmly. "Oh. Someone else will be here, too. Evelyn Daiches will be up for a couple of days."

Dan waited for a response, but none came. "Well?"

"It's your party, Dan." Alex tried, unsuccessfully, to sound diplomatic.

"Do you disapprove, Alex?"

After a few moments' silence, Alex said quietly, "It's not that I *disapprove*, Dan, it's... Look, I'll talk with you when I get there."

Dan felt peeved at Alex's suspense ploy. "Really, Alex. If you don't approve of my seeing Evelyn, why don't you tell me so? You can join the Greek chorus when you arrive."

"Look, Dan, as I said before, that's your affair. If you'd rather, I'll not come." His tone was serious.

Dan was startled. "Oh, Alex, don't be silly. I'm just stupidly defensive about Evelyn for some reason. Perhaps you can talk some sense into me."

Alex sighed into the receiver. "Ah, Daniel, Daniel." He paused. "Well, Dan, my mother is frantically signaling me to end this call. I'll see you on the thirty-first."

"I'm looking forward to it, Alex," Dan said warmly.

"Goodbye, then."

"Goodbye."

Dan stood for a few moments with his hand resting on the replaced receiver, pondering the imperfection of the telephone. Why had Alex been so ambiguous about Evelyn Daiches? Had Manetti phoned him and muttered threats against Dan? Perhaps that girl he'd been with at Honeywell's party. Perhaps that hadn't worked out. Or perhaps she'd told Alex something about Evelyn. Something unpleasant.

He grew disgusted with himself for allowing people to manipulate him into having petty suspicions about Evelyn. What bothered him most was the grain of truth at the core of everyone's argument. He really didn't know Evelyn. All he knew was how she kissed his face again and again when he brought her to orgasm.

Of such stuff are fools made. This he knew.

XXXII

In the afternoon, Manetti called. It was not a friendly conversation. Manetti's boorish temperament Dan found irksome. The end of the conversation (at least the part before Dan hung up on Manetti) was especially senseless and vicious.

"Will you make your point?" Dan asked, annoyed at Manetti's blustering.

"The point is, asshole, that *you've* been sleeping in *my* bed. Eating *my* honey. Maybe I give people a taste sometimes, but I don't let them keep it. I'm going to get you for this," Manetti growled.

Dan ignored the obvious inconsistency of Manetti's food metaphor as well as his bluster. "Did I understand you to say that *I've* been sleeping in *your* bed? Eating *your* honey?" he regretted that Manetti was unable to see his smirk.

"That's what I said."

"Well, then," Dan said calmly, "I guess that makes me something of a Goldilocks, doesn't it?" Dan felt like a matador shaking the red cape.

"Deal, you mother—"

Dan hung up the phone. He wished he'd had a snappy response, but he reasoned that a half-veronica was better than nothing.

XXXIII

Ramona scrupulously avoided being alone with Dan for the rest of the afternoon, confirming his suspicion that she had told Grandfather Deal of his relationship with Alicia Pauls. He busied himself getting things ready for the visits of Evelyn and Alex. He chose the bedroom opposite his own for Evelyn, the one by the bathroom, opposite Ramona's room, for Alex. Maisie helped him make up the beds and put out towels and extra blankets.

He was alone in the study reading when Ramona came in. "May I talk with you?" she asked, shyly approaching him.

He had dragged his chair near the fireplace and had his shoes off letting the fire warm his feet. He hoped Evelyn didn't mind cold bedrooms.

"Surely," he replied. He continued to read.

Ramona was not deterred by his rudeness. She took a seat on the ottoman he'd left behind when he'd moved his chair and scooted over beside him. She rested her elbows on the arm of his chair and cupped her chin in her hands.

"I told Grandfather about you and Alicia," she said quietly.

Dan looked coolly at her. "I had assumed as much."

He resumed his reading.

"What are you reading?" She tipped the book up so that she could see its spine. "Oh. *Robinson Crusoe*. I thought it might be something spicier."

Dan frowned at her. "I do not think about, nor do I wish to read about, sex all the time, despite what you have made Grandfather believe." He went back to reading.

Ramona stood. Dan glanced up at her, then returned to his book. He had no intention of being intimidated by such an obvious act of domination.

"What *I've* made Grandfather believe!" she cried. "Let me tell you something, Daniel Randolph Deal. I didn't volunteer that information. Grandfather practically forced it out of me. Daddy and Uncle Charles went bird hunting out at the farm the day before Christmas. They ate lunch at the cabin, and Uncle Charles found a pair of women's gloves on the table. He brought them back here the day after Christmas and asked if they were mine. When I said they weren't, Uncle Charles told Grandfather that he thought someone was 'meeting a woman,' as he put it, out at the farm."

"I can imagine," Dan said, smiling absently.

Ramona sat down again and took one of Dan's hands in her two. "Anyway," she continued confidentially, "Grandfather asked him if they had seen any signs of people coming and going. Daddy said he didn't recall any. Then Uncle Charles said something about your having been out there December twenty-third. Grandfather then cleared his throat in that way he has that lets everyone know that he wants to change the subject, so Daddy and Uncle Charles simply let the matter drop. Then, next day, the snow had cleared enough so that Uncle Charles could take Daddy and Mother home in his Jeep."

"I bet Grandfather loved having everyone here," Dan said quietly.

Ramona nodded. "Of course," she added, "he missed you."

Dan studied her face for some hint of her intention. He thought perhaps she'd meant the comment as an insinuation, but she showed no sign of having meant it so.

"And after the others left?" he asked.

She shrugged. "Grandfather brought me in here and quizzed me about you and Alicia Pauls. He specifically wanted to know if you had gone out with Alicia the same night that you stayed out at the cabin. I had to admit that you had, Dan. I could never lie to Grandfather."

"Nor would I want you to." He squeezed her hand.

"So you see, Dan, I didn't tattle to Grandfather about you and Alicia. I wouldn't do that. Alicia is no threat."

She looked at him earnestly for a few moments, then sat up and released his hand from hers. Her features relaxed visibly and she said lightly, "What I mean is, I know you're not in love with her."

Dan closed his book and massaged his face. "So. Grandfather found me out."

He shook his head and watched the fire. "Just as well. That relationship has never been fair to Alicia, anyway."

"She seems to have liked i," Ramona said coyly. She looked at the fire, then back at him. "What are you going to do, Dan?"

"Well, I told Grandfather, at least I implied to him, that I was going to break off with Alicia. And, like you, I would never lie to him."

Ramona looked surprised. "What about... Evelyn?"

Dan looked straight into her eyes. "Grandfather and I discussed her, too. I told him that Evelyn and I were... were more serious."

Ramona flinched and Dan was taken aback. He had never before considered her attachment to him. He had always considered that part of their relationship a wonderful secret that they shared. He thought she must realize the impossibility of their attraction reaching fruition.

Suddenly her eyes went opaque. It was a skill she'd had since childhood. He knew he'd see no more.

"How will you handle, Alicia?" she asked calmly.

He wrinkled his brow. "Badly, I'm sure. But it will have to be done."

Ramona stood abruptly. "Well. I need to go see if Maisie needs any help with dinner."

Dan sensed a tear in their relationship, but he felt helpless to do anything about it.

"Is something wrong, Ramona?" he asked. The insipidity of his question made him look away from her in embarrassment.

"No," she said shortly, then went to the door.

She turned back to say something. Dan looked closely at her; her eyes glistened as if the firelight reflected tears.

"I'll call you when dinner's ready," she said.

Then she was gone.

Dan stared at the empty doorway for a few moments, then turned back to Robinson Crusoe's struggles. They seemed easier than his.

XXXIV

Dinner was funereal. Grandfather Deal ate in silence, nodding or shaking his head in response to Ramona's proffers of food.

Ramona was subdued, brightening when she tried to serve Grandfather, lapsing into pensiveness as she picked at her own food.

Although he was hungry, Dan didn't eat much because he hesitated to disturb the gloom by asking for food.

Finally Dan gave up and excused himself. Later that night, alone in his frigid room, New Year's Eve seemed a long time away.

XXXV

During breakfast the next morning, Dan mentioned going to Roanoke to look at the Randolph house. It was something he did every year during the Christmas holidays, a sort of pilgrimage to the wellspring of his Southern gentility and pride.

Although his tone was rather formal and distant, Grandfather Deal approved his plans and Dan knew that he was forgiven, at least in some way.

Ramona excused herself from the table upon hearing his plans. She had an animated conversation with someone, evidently a girlfriend, because the few snatches of conversation that Dan and his Grandfather Deal overheard (purely by accident, of course) concerned a male: "You'll know him, he's the same." Followed shortly after by, "Of course you can. He's a man, isn't he?"

Dan caught his grandfather's eye, and they smiled at each other. Their insulated lives as men made the machinations of women seem all the more amusing to them.

When Ramona came back to the table, she was all bright looks and teasing comments to both of them. Dan was relieved to see the previous day's clouds lifting.

Dan drove over to Roanoke after breakfast. At Ramona's suggestion he stopped by the Roanoke Historical Society's offices to pick up a map of historic homes decorated for the holidays.

It was there he met Audrey Robinson, a girl he'd known in high school who'd attended Roanoke College and who worked for the Historical Society. She had been a cheerleading mentor of Ramona's, so they chatted about how Ramona was and what they were each doing.

At her insistence, Dan allowed her to chauffeur him around Roanoke. She had to visit several of the historical sites on Society business. Dan saw several examples of antebellum and Victorian architecture while Audrey saw to her affairs.

At about twelve-thirty she suggested that they go to lunch. Dan, flattered by the attentions of a girl he'd always thought of as beautiful and seen as unattainable, hungry in the bargain, readily concurred.

Jim Booth

She took him to a Greek restaurant in the cellar of a downtown storefront. They had Greek salad and souvlaki, rather garlicky, which led to each making flirty comments about being unkissable. Audrey insisted that the draft beer was superb and ordered a pitcher of that. Since she was talkative, Dan found himself listening, and drinking, more than he was used to. Each time his glass got half-empty, Audrey refilled it for him.

At the end of the meal, she excused herself to call her office. Dan went to the restroom. When he returned to the table, she was waiting for him, her coat already on, a bag of something in her hand. She had already paid the bill. Dan offered her money, but she declined it saying that she'd treat it as a business lunch and be reimbursed. She helped Dan into his coat, and they went out to her car.

"Would you mind going with me to my apartment, Dan?" she asked. "I need to check on my cat."

The beer he'd drunk had made Dan mellow and agreeable, so the idea was fine by him. On the way to her place, Audrey stopped at a convenience store and bought a six-pack of beer. Dan, at her gentle prodding, had one in the car on the way to her place.

Her apartment was a large duplex, the upper floor of a huge two-story home in a section of Roanoke much like the section of Lynchburg where Dan lived. Dan expressed his liking for the place as they climbed the stairs to her outside entrance.

"I picked this place because I've always loved your home, Dan," she said as she unlocked the door and motioned him in. "It's a bit more expensive than I'd like, but I really enjoy the space." She hesitated, then added, as if the information were confidential, "And the sense of superiority it gives me."

Dan went over and looked out a front window while Audrey hung up their coats and went to the kitchen. He turned as she re-entered the room, and she smiled at him and held out another beer. He went to her, took it, and began to drink automatically.

"Here, Dan," she said, guiding him to the sofa, "relax for a few minutes."

"It's a lovely apartment, Audrey. You have excellent taste." He sat down on the horsehair sofa and slipped off his loafers. He rested his stocking feet on the old trunk she used as a coffee table and let his beer rest on his stomach.

It was a very nice room, decorated with carefully chosen pieces of Blue Ridge folk art and furnished with nicely refurbished pieces such as the sofa on which he relaxed.

Audrey sat down very close to him and slipped off her shoes. She drew her feet up under her.

"Do you really like it?" she asked eagerly. "Monty thinks it's horrible. He wants to know why I don't get some new furniture instead of always buying old junk that somebody's fixed up." She opened her own beer and took a sip.

Dan, who had been studying the label on his beer can, looked at her incredulously. "Monty Land? You still see Monty Land?"

Her high school sweetheart. A football star in high school, a player of no note at Virginia Tech. He'd joined his father's Chevrolet dealership after graduation.

"We were engaged until a couple of months ago when I found out he was cheating on me. So I called it off." She took a long pull at her beer, then sighed. "He's been bugging me to give him another chance." Another long drink. "Maybe I'll give him one after New Year's." After a moment she added, "Unless something better comes along."

"Why give him another chance?" Dan put his feet back on the floor and carefully set his beer on the coffee table. Everything felt warm and pleasant.

"Because he's pretty good in bed," Audrey said languorously. She turned and lay back on the sofa, her head in Dan's lap. She put her beer on the floor. Her long, beautiful chestnut colored hair, which hung nearly to her waist, trailed over his legs.

Careful not to disturb Audrey's head or upset his beer, Dan put his feet back on the coffee table. He looked down at the beautiful woman who had her head in his lap, not certain how he had come to be in his present circumstance, glad that he was.

"Monty Land is a football playing clod with no breeding. You can do better," he said for no reason.

Audrey reached up and stroked his face.

He leaned over her and took up a handful of her lovely hair and rubbed it against his cheek.

She sat up slowly, and, placing her own beer carefully on the coffee table, took him by the hand and led him to her bedroom, stopping along the way to kiss him two or three times.

Her bed was a beautifully refinished oak four-poster.

Jim Booth

They were most comfortable there.

XXXVI

When Dan awoke, it was after six and dark outside. He could hear a subdued bustling in another room and Joni Mitchell's voice coming from somewhere. Between the lovemaking and the sleep, he felt largely sobered. The bed was warm and smelled of Audrey.

As he lay there, warm and indolent, it occurred to him that Alex would think him a madman. Here he was getting involved with another woman when he already had Evelyn and Ramona making his life complicated, to say nothing of Alicia Pauls, with whom he would have a difficult time breaking off.

Audrey came in wearing a peach colored terry cloth robe and fuzzy slippers, her hair brushed and shining. She carried a tray on which sat a teapot, two mugs, and a small plate of baklava. That must have been what she had in the bag from the restaurant.

Dan smiled at her warmly and genuinely. It seemed to him that there could be nothing more warm and pleasing than having a woman wait upon him after he had made love to her.

He sat up in bed and propped himself against the headboard, his pillow behind his head. Audrey put the tray on his lap and took off her robe, smiling shyly at him as she did so. Then she walked around the bed and got in beside him. Her hand touched his leg.

"I made tea because I know you prefer it," she said, propping herself with pillows and snuggling close to him.

Surprised, Dan turned to her. "How do you know that?"

She smiled shyly. "Don't you remember, Dan? We had that student council breakfast at the Holiday Inn and you got into an argument with the waitress because you ordered tea and she kept bringing everyone else coffees and not bringing you tea? Don't you remember what you said to her? People talked about it for days."

"Only the uncivilized drink coffee,'" Dan said, smiling ruefully. "What a pompous ass I was."

"Oh, no, Dan, you were wonderful. All the girls had crushes on you." Dan turned to her and Audrey blushed becomingly and looked away coyly.

163

Dan shook his head. "Yes, I'm sure they did. That's why I went alone to the senior prom."

"Did you ask anyone?" Audrey smiled shyly.

Feeling foolish, Dan looked down at the tray. "No." His tender ego prevented him–for fear of what he felt would be certain, repeated refusals. "I didn't think anyone would go with me." He looked up, startled at himself for voicing such an admission.

"Oh, Dan. I would have gone with you." Her voice dripped sincerity.

Dan smiled wanly. "And Monty Land would have caught me in a parking lot somewhere and beaten me up." He smiled slyly at her. "As I recall," he said, measuring his words for dramatic effect, "you and Ramona used to show up at my grandfather's pretty often, didn't you?"

She smiled and dropped her eyes.

Dan continued, half in jest, half in hope, "Did *you* have a crush on me?"

Audrey avoided his eyes. She leaned over and poured tea for both of them. Dan began to think he'd been ungentlemanly. He was about to apologize when she spoke.

"Yes, Dan," she said, looking up at him as she handed him a mug of tea, "I did have a crush on you. And on your grandfather, and on your house, and on your name." She picked up her own mug and looked at it thoughtfully. "You're descended from the Randolphs, Dan." She looked at him, her face serious.

"Yes, there's aristocratic blood flowing through these veins," Dan said lightly. "But don't let's talk about that. Let's go back to the subject of your crush on me." He waggled his eyebrows, hoping to shake her serious mien.

"But that's you, Dan. You're a gentleman. A Southern gentleman. You were born one, and you've been bred one by your grandfather. There aren't many left." Her voice was soft but adamant.

Dan sighed and held out his mug in a toast. "To the South, ma'am."

She smiled, a little wistfully, and clinked her mug against his. They sipped their tea.

As he looked at her through the steam rising from her mug, Audrey seemed far away. Dan's spirits fell suddenly. "Let's have some baklava," he said quietly. He handed her a pastry.

"Dan?"

"Yes?"

"Would you mind if I were forward?" It seemed an odd question from a woman whom he had known only casually and who had taken him to bed at their first meeting in nearly two years.

"No. Not at all." He smiled. "Be as forward as you like."

She smiled in return. "Good. Well, I'd like to take you out New Year's Eve. I've got tickets for a big bash at the Civic Center." She leaned over confidentially. "If you could arrange to stay over, I know where you could find a warm place to sleep."

Always complications. He felt he should be honest with her. "I... I have friends coming, from out of town. They'll be here tomorrow. We already have plans for the evening."

"Oh. I see." She shrugged. "May I be forward again?"

"Please do."

"Are any of these friends... female?" she asked hesitantly.

He sighed. "Yes," he said, nodding. He didn't know how much to tell her.

She sat there expectant, beautiful; her rich brown eyes fixed on him.

He realized suddenly that Evelyn meant nothing to him. He wished Audrey would say something so he might know how to proceed.

"Is the female, special?" she asked.

"Well..." he began.

Audrey looked pained.

He tried again. "We've been seeing each other this semester at Wake Forest." Her look made him add hastily, "Not a lot. But we have..." He groped for language. "Become close," he finished awkwardly.

She looked confused—and a little sad, he thought, so he tried again.

"What I mean is, we're not seeing each other exclusively." She cut her eyes at him, and he hesitated, realizing he was articulating the obvious. "But we are... have been, seeing more of each other than anyone else. I spent a couple of days there after Christmas... due to the snow."

Wrong. All wrong.

He sighed. "We're... I'm not really sure where we stand, Audrey. At least, not now." He felt confused, and disgusted with himself. "There's no good explanation," he said, more to himself than to her.

She put her mug back on the tray. She took his mug, put it on the tray, then took the tray from him and set it on the floor beside the bed. She snuggled down in the covers and held out her arms.

"Do you want to talk about it?" she asked gently.

He went into her arms and told her everything, just as if she were Ramona. She listened gently, stroking his hair, his head upon her breast.

Dan felt a great sense of relief from being perfectly honest and open.

"When will she go home?" she asked when he'd finished.

"The second of January."

"When do you go back to school?" She traced a finger down his chest and made his stomach muscles quiver.

"The tenth."

She turned his face to hers. "Do you want to see me again, Dan?"

He pulled her to him. "Very much, Audrey. Very much."

She smiled, unashamedly pleased. "This isn't a fair place to have this conversation, is it?"

He shrugged. "As fair a place as for me to confess other amours to you."

They smiled at each other. Dan felt happy, even a little giddy. He wondered if the beer were still affecting him.

"Speaking of amour," she said coyly, "how about a little more?"

Dan's sense of honor suddenly, strangely, kicked in. "I... I don't know what's going to happen with this other thing," he said solemnly.

Audrey nuzzled against him and kissed his throat, then began working her way down his torso, kissing as she went. "The other thing..." (Kiss) "Seems pretty far..." (Kiss) "Away..." (Kiss) "Right now..." (Kiss) "Doesn't it?"

"Yes. Yes it does. Oh, yes. Yes."

Her head popped out from under the bedclothes. "You haven't said when you'll see me again." She smiled. "I'm being unfair again. On purpose."

Dan rolled her over and looked down at her. "Is the night of January second all right?" He began kissing her as she'd been kissing him.

"Yes. Yes, that's good. Oh, yes, that's so good."

XXXVII

It was bitterly cold when Audrey took Dan back to his car, which was still parked at the historical society's office. An Arctic cold front was pushing south from Canada. They heard on the radio that the temperature would be in single digits by morning. Dan asked Audrey to wait until he got his car started because he wasn't sure his battery would work properly.

It worked fine. He left his engine running as he went over to Audrey's car to tell her goodbye one last time. She rolled down her window.

"Here." She handed him a folded piece of paper.

"What's this?"

"My address and phone number. I drew a little map so you can find my place."

Dan unfolded the paper and studied the map briefly. It was extraordinarily clear. "If I get lost I'll call you," he said, knowing he could get to her house in his sleep.

"It's freezing out. Come around and get in." She rolled up her window.

"I can't," Dan said through the glass. "I'm low on gas and I need to get going to find a service station."

"What?" she called through the glass.

He went around and got in. "I can only stay a second. I'm low on gas, and I've got to find a service station."

A pause.

"Kiss me goodbye again," she said. He did. A shiver ran through him. The cold, he thought.

"I've got to go," he said.

"Dan, do come back."

"On the second. As I promised."

"If you can't make it, call and let me know." She squeezed his hand, and he knew then that everything that had happened had been a risk she'd taken. For him.

"I'll be here," he said in his most gentlemanly, most reassuring tone. He kissed her cheek. She clung to him for a moment.

"Drive carefully, darling," she said.

"You, too. Goodbye."

"Goodbye, Dan."

He got out and she drove slowly away, turning awkwardly to wave to him as she went. He walked to his car and got in. As he turned his car around and headed for the interstate, it seemed important to look at the map to Audrey's house again.

He drew what he thought was the paper from his coat pocket, but it turned out to be the note Evelyn had written and put in with the sandwiches her mother had given him.

He crumpled the paper and threw it out the window.

XXXVIII

"What time did you get back from Roanoke, Daniel?" asked Grandfather Deal. He sat at the breakfast table stirring his coffee and looking at his grandson.

Dan poured syrup lavishly onto his pancakes. "About eleven last night, sir. It was somewhat past ten when I left Roanoke."

Grandfather Deal sipped his coffee. "I wouldn't have thought the Randolph House stayed open so late. You did go to the Randolph House did you not?" he said deliberately.

"Yes sir." Dan took a bite and chewed slowly to give himself time to think about how to broach the subject of Audrey. A flank attack seemed advantageous, so he turned to Ramona. "I ran into a friend of yours, Ramona," he said, turning to his cousin. "Audrey Robinson. She works for the Roanoke Historical Society. She went to school with me. I think she helped coach you when you were a jayvee cheerleader."

"Later on, too," said Ramona. "When she was at Roanoke College. We got to be friends." Ramona smiled at her coffee. She knew she'd outmaneuvered him.

Dan watched her for a moment, unable to fathom her Cheshire cat behavior, then turned back to his grandfather. "Anyway, sir, Audrey was nice enough to take me around with her as she was visiting various historical sites about the city. Part of her job."

He stopped and took a long drink of his tea. "Maisie, do you think I could have another cup of tea this morning?"

"Surely, Daniel." She got up from the table where she'd only just gotten seated and went to the kitchen. As she returned with the kettle and a fresh tea bag, Dan continued his story.

"So, Audrey took me out for lunch. Then we went by her apartment." He paused and smiled at his grandfather's look of surprise and at the old man's involuntary glances at Ramona and Maisie. "So that she could feed her cat. She showed me some of the Blue Ridge folk art she's collected."

Grandfather Deal sat back in his chair and crossed his arms, waiting.

171

"Anyway, she'd bought my lunch, so I insisted on buying her dinner, and of course I had to wait around until time for that. Then when we were at dinner we were talking and time got away from us." Dan paused because Grandfather Deal was clearing his throat, a signal that he wanted the floor.

"Is this the young lady who came here with you rather frequently, Ramona?" he asked.

"Yes, Grandfather. She went to Roanoke College, then she got a job in Roanoke and just stayed over there. I think she wanted to go to Hollins but couldn't get in." Ramona looked at Dan as she made the last statement.

Grandfather dabbed at the corners of his mouth with his napkin, then said, "Well, as I remember her, she was a sweet young lady. Very refined and mannerly. And you say you and she spent the day together, Daniel?" He took up his coffee and sipped it, still watching his grandson.

"Yes sir, we did. It was most enjoyable. She is, as you say, a very sweet girl." Dan pushed away his plate and took up his tea.

Grandfather Deal set his cup in its saucer. "Well, I've not done my morning reading. I believe I'll go to the study, if you all will excuse me." He rose from the table carefully. Ramona and Dan watched him leave the room in his inimitably dignified manner. Maisie began to bustle about clearing away dishes.

"So. You ran into Audrey Robinson." Ramona tapped her coffee cup with her fingernail.

"Yes, I did. She was quite refreshing, too, after some of the women I've had to deal with of late." Dan sipped his tea contentedly.

Ramona smiled mischievously. "Did she tell you I'd called her?"

Dan put his cup down so hard it clattered the saucer. "What?"

"I called her. Yesterday morning. After you said you were going to look at the old Randolph house again. I told her to be on the lookout for you. And I sent you to the historical society's office to make sure you'd meet her." Ramona took a sip of coffee, then set her cup down. Silently. "Tell me," she continued, looking at Dan amusedly, "did you notice her, or did she notice you?"

He nodded resignedly. "She noticed me. Part of your master plan, I suppose?"

"Yes, indeed," Ramona said lightly. Then her expression became serious and she added, "Daniel, Audrey is **really** interested in you. She's carried a torch for you since high school. When she found out about you and Alicia Pauls, she cried for a whole day."

"How, when, and where did she 'find out' about me and Alicia Pauls?" Dan asked pointedly.

"Oh, that's not important. I told her, of course. I was sorry for it later, when I saw how it hurt her. That was years ago. Dan, I believe she cares for you. As much as I do."

"And?" He sipped his tea.

"And if I can't have you, I'd rather she did than anyone else." Ramona leaned across the table and held out her hand. Dan took it. "Don't you think she's sweet, Dan?" she asked gently.

Dan looked into his cousin's china blue eyes. "Possibly as sweet as you," he said.

It was then that Ramona realized she could never have him. It was then she let go. "You'll never have blue-eyed children," she said wistfully. "Audrey's eyes are brown."

He laughed softly. "Ramona, dear, you're incorrigible. I'm not going to have any children with anybody for a long, long time."

Ramona took away her hand. "Are you going to see Audrey again?"

Dan smiled mischievously. As if she doubted that he would. "Of course. On the second of January. She invited me out for this evening, but, as you well know, I have other plans."

She frowned.

"Ramona, one does not simply break previously made engagements for one's convenience, no matter what one's desire might be," he added sternly.

Maisie came from the kitchen to take away their cups. Ramona and Dan waited silently as she took them and went from the room. "Dan, would you rather go out with Audrey, or Evelyn?" Ramona asked as soon as the kitchen door had stopped swinging.

"It's not a question of that. It's a question of doing the right thing. 'Noblesse oblige.'"

"As Grandfather would say," Ramona said evenly, "it would be ungentlemanly of you to break your date with Evelyn."

"Exactly."

"God, Dan." Ramona leaned back in her chair and crossed her arms. "Do you *really* believe that nonsense?"

Incredulous, Dan replied, "Of course, I do."

She sighed. "Then you must be what Audrey claims you are." She stood. Dan stood also. They walked to the dining room door.

"What does Audrey claim that I am?" Dan asked, trying to appear only politely curious.

"A Southern gentleman."

Dan bowed and motioned for her to precede him from the room. "After you, ma'am," he drawled.

Ramona leaned over and kissed the top of his head. "Thank you, sir."

As they made their way down the hall, Dan gave her a flattering portrait of Alex Radford.

XXXIX

Alex arrived first, just before lunch.

"You must have left Lightfoot quite early," Dan said as he helped his friend carry in his bags.

"Not as early as you might think, Daniel. The interstate highway system is a monument to American ingenuity and efficiency. I-64 west to U.S. 29 south and here I am." Alex smiled and betrayed his facetious intent.

"Most efficiently done, I'd say." Dan smiled in return as they went into the house, at Alex's insistence, through the back door. Maisie was in the kitchen making a cake. Daniel started to introduce her, but Alex interrupted.

"Why, Daniel," he said, winking broadly, "you didn't tell me that Ramona could cook, too." Maisie's hands were flour covered, but Alex insisted on kissing one of them, getting flour on his face in the process.

"You're a charmer," Maisie said as she handed him a towel. He dabbed at his face.

"Strange," he said, suddenly looking serious.

"What?" asked Maisie.

"That's what I was going to tell you." He winked at her and she shooed him away.

"Take this charming rogue out of my kitchen, Daniel, or I'll never get lunch finished," she said.

Dan opened the door to the dining room. "Forth, Casanova. There are other conquests to be made."

They made their way through the dining room and down the front hall toward the stairs. At the door of the study Dan stopped and looked in. Ramona was sitting in an easy chair near the fireplace, her feet propped on an ottoman, reading a magazine.

"Is that Ramona?" Alex asked in a stage whisper. Ramona looked up. Alex pushed past Dan and crossed the room to her theatrically. When he reached her side, he made a courtly bow.

"Wythe Alexander Radford, ma'am," he said. He still had a bit of flour on his nose. "Defender of the weak, admirer of beauty, Southern gentleman. At your service, ma'am." He took up her hand and kissed it, in the process leaving the flour on her.

Ramona looked from Alex to Dan and back again. "What is this?" she asked dubiously. Then she caught sight of the flour on her hand. "And, what is *this*?"

"That, ma'am, is a treasure I have carried here to greet you with, fair flower of the South," Alex said quickly and with bravado. "I have brought you this." He hesitated a moment, then added, "Flour. Flour for the flower of the South."

He took her hand and studied it. "Yet, now I see I was wrong to do this," he added gravely.

"Why?" asked Ramona, taken in just like Maisie.

"Because, my dear," he said, turning and winking at Dan, "your beauty is so great it eclipses that of this... mere flour."

Ramona laughed, genuinely pleased.

Dan laughed, too, although not quite sure at what. Alex was certainly being glib and charming; a little too much so for Dan's reserved nature. He attributed it to nervousness.

Suddenly Alex let go of Ramona's hand. He took a handkerchief from his pocket and rubbed his face.

It was then that Dan realized his grandfather had been standing behind him; for how long he didn't know.

Grandfather Deal stepped past Dan into the room. Alex put away his handkerchief and went to him, hand extended. "My name is Alex Radford. Honored to meet you, sir," he added, all politesse.

"Forgive me, Grandfather," said Dan, stepping forward. "I should introduce you all properly." He stepped past his grandfather and stood just to one side of the pair. "Grandfather, allow me to introduce Mr.. Wythe Alexander Radford of Lightfoot, Virginia. Alex, this is my grandfather, Augustus Stuart Deal III of Lynchburg."

"A pleasure, sir." Alex nodded neatly.

"Honored, sir." Grandfather did the same.

They shook hands again. "Grandfather," Dan interrupted, "I need to take Alex up to his room so that he can freshen up for lunch."

"Certainly." Grandfather Deal nodded again at Alex. "We'll talk again at lunch, Mr.–"

"Alex, please, sir," Alex interposed.

"At lunch, then, Alex." Grandfather nodded to the two as they left him. At the door Alex stopped.

"Miss Ramona, I go to prepare myself to worship at the shrine of your beauty." He grinned and ducked out the door.

Ramona looked at Dan. "Is he always like this?"

Dan smiled and shrugged. "I'd say he's in rare form today."

"Ah, and what is so rare as a day in June... or rather, December?" came from the hall.

"He seems to have a sprightly wit," observed Grandfather Deal quietly.

"Yes sir," Dan said and excused himself again.

Alex was sitting on the stairs with his bags, waiting patiently. Dan showed him up to his room and pointed out the bathroom.

"Hope your grandfather wasn't put off by my little scene with Ramona," Alex said as he came back into his room where Dan waited.

"No, I don't believe so," Dan said, watching his friend as he combed his hair with his fingers in front of the dresser mirror. "Grandfather said you have a sprightly wit. He rarely comments on people unless he approves of them. He's very much of the old school."

"Well, I'm glad I didn't offend him." He turned to Dan and smiled. "Do you think I put Ramona off?" He went over and sat down by Dan on the bed and leaned back, propping himself on his elbows.

Dan wrinkled his brow. "She's intrigued, I think." Then, more seriously, "It might be a good idea to be more subdued at lunch, though. Grandfather likes his sprightliness in small doses."

Alex nodded, then stood. "Shall we go down, then?"

"Certainly."

They went down to find the others already at the table. Alex was more subdued, as Dan had suggested, but still entertaining. His manner with Grandfather Deal was respectful and engaging at once.

Dan was quiet through the meal, content to let Alex carry the burden of table talk. Women wandered through his thoughts: Evelyn, Ramona, Alicia Pauls, and Audrey. He made a mental note to call Alicia and arrange a meeting so as to break with her. At least, he thought, that situation could be resolved in some fashion. As for the others, he felt that perhaps the next few days might give him some idea how to proceed.

It was a relaxed and enjoyable table gathering, the first completely so since Grandfather had confronted Dan about Alicia. Dan watched Ramona briefly. Not without a twinge did he notice that she seemed quite taken with Alex. It occurred to him then that things might already be working themselves out.

XXXX

Evelyn called from a service station at an exit off U.S. 29. Her fan belt had broken, and her car had overheated.

"The attendant says he'll have to let the car cool down before he can fix it," she said, her voice shrill above the noise of the service station. "He says it's too hot to handle right now. La voiture et la chauffeureuse sont les mêmes, n'est pas?" Her laugh through the telephone receiver tickled Dan's ear and made him shiver.

"How far away are you?" he asked quietly. "I could come out and get you, and we could pick up the car tomorrow."

"What's wrong?" Alex asked, standing at Dan's elbow as he talked on the phone by the stairs at the front of the house. "Evelyn can't make it?"

Dan held up his hand to quiet him. "What's that? About fifteen miles out? Exit 116. Texaco station. All right, I'll be out to pick you up as soon as I can. What? Yes, you, too, dear. Goodbye."

He put the receiver in its cradle and turned to Alex. "Evelyn's car lost its fan belt out on Highway 29. I'll have to drive out and pick her up. Why don't you and Ramona go ahead and get ready for the evening so that when we get back Evelyn and I can shower and change. Our dinner reservations are for seven-thirty and it's five-twenty now."

"Where's Dan going?" Ramona leaned over the banister.

Alex started to speak, but Ramona began again. "Oh, I know," she said facetiously, turning to Dan. "That was Evelyn on the phone. She can't make it, so you're going to go to Roanoke, pick up Audrey, then hustle back here so we can all have dinner together before you and she hustle off to that society thing she was telling me about this morning."

"Who's Audrey?" asked Alex.

"You talked to Audrey this morning?" Dan reached up and took hold of two banister uprights. "What did she have to say? Who is she taking to the New Year's Eve celebration?"

Ramona leaned farther over the railing. "No one. She said if she couldn't take the man she wanted, she'd go alone."

"Is that true, Ramona?" Dan looked at her, dubious.

"Yes." Ramona looked steadily at him.

"Ramona?"

"Yes?"

"Could *you* explain who Audrey is?" Alex went around and climbed the stairs, stopping just below Ramona.

"I'll tell you later," she said. Her tone suggested that "later" could be anywhere. She and Alex looked at each other, their eyes communicating, in Ramona's case something she wanted to feel, in Alex's, something he felt he dared not say.

Dan reached out and tapped her foot. "Ramona?"

"Yes, dear," she said absently, languorously, her eyes still on Alex.

"I have to go out to a service station and pick up Evelyn. She had car trouble. That's what the phone call was about."

She frowned and shrugged out of her languor. "Damn."

"Now, now, let's not become sullen," said Alex. He leaned over the banister beside her. "You'd better hurry, Dan," he said glancing at his watch. "It's five-thirty."

He turned back to Ramona. "Who's Audrey?"

Dan left them standing there, Ramona enumerating the virtues of her friend, Alex leaning on the banister looking up at her earnestly. As he went through the kitchen, Grandfather Deal and Maisie were discussing the comparative virtues of pecan and pumpkin pie.

"Where are you off to?" asked Grandfather, surprised. "Isn't your friend supposed to arrive any minute?"

Dan explained briefly her plight and his errand of assistance.

"Very gentlemanly, Daniel. You hurry along and bring that girl back here so we can meet her," said Maisie.

Grandfather Deal picked up the sifter, but Maisie took it from him and began snowing flour into a large bowl.

Dan shook his head at them, then went out to fetch Evelyn.

XXXXI

It took him nearly thirty minutes to reach the service station, so it was a quarter-past-six when Evelyn kissed him on the cheek as he carried her bags to his car.

"We must hurry," he told her. "We have a dinner reservation at seven-thirty and I'm sure you'll want to shower and change before we go out--after being in the car, I mean."

She smiled. It was pleasant to see him make a faux pas.

"Is it far to your house?" she asked, peeking around the car's trunk lid at him.

"Just about a half hour." He closed the trunk. "I'll just let the attendant know when you'll be back for the car." Dan started toward the station.

"Wait!"

Dan turned back to her.

"I... I've already told him I'd pick up the car tomorrow. Let's hurry to your house. I want to make myself beautiful for you."

She smiled at him, but Dan merely nodded and went round to his side of the car. They got in and started for Lynchburg.

While they had been moving the bags, there had been no time for talk. Enclosed in the car with her, Dan knew he must say something. He had thought that seeing her would allay some of the sense of distance that the previous evening had created. It did not. They rode in silence for four or five miles.

His right hand rested on the gearshift. She put her left on top of it. "I'm glad to be here," she said timidly, giving his hand a squeeze.

"It's nice of you to come," Dan said, sounding, to himself, very formal and insincere.

He downshifted to pass a truck that was struggling up a grade, and she was forced to remove her hand from his. They reached the hilltop and sped down as he let his foot lie heavy on the accelerator.

"Are we in a hurry?" she asked.

Dan glanced at her, but she had turned her head and was looking out the window.

181

"I just don't want to be late." He pressed the gas pedal harder.

"You seem as if you just want to get it over with."

To Dan, her voice sounded petulant. He sighed in response. They rode in silence for a few more minutes.

"Evelyn?" he said quietly.

"Yes?"

"I... I've been seeing someone else." Telling her seemed the only fair thing to do.

She exhaled, a little brokenly, Dan thought.

"Oh."

Then she ventured, her voice noncommittal, "An old flame?"

He wondered how to answer her. "Something like that," he said finally.

She turned to him and put her hand on his arm. "I could... I could go back and wait for the car." Best to find out where she stood.

"Don't be silly," he said, watching the road instead of looking at her. "I invited you here." He glanced at her and added, "Besides, people are expecting you."

She looked out the window at the darkness. God, he could be a pompous bastard. She decided to hold herself in check. If he were this fickle, it might be because he was confused. He liked demure and sad. She'd give him that.

"It's very cold here, isn't it?" she said feelingly.

"It certainly is," Dan replied lightly.

He leapt at the opportunity to make small talk. "This Arctic cold front is supposed to linger for another couple of days. The high temperature today was only thirty degrees."

He was enjoying the meaninglessness of the talk when she interrupted.

Pitching her voice at what she thought would be a tone just short of insinuation, she said, "It'll be cold while I'm up here."

Dan decided that the best way to treat such an obviously pregnant remark would be with an innocuously sterile reply.

"Ah, no, not at all," he said pleasantly. "Grandfather's house is warm, and we can sit by the fire while I read to you. Or we can talk to Ramona and Alex."

She started, visibly, in spite of herself. "Alex Radford?" She wondered if her voice trembled.

Dan took note but gave no sign of recognition.

"Yes. He's my housemate, as you know. He's here for a couple of days. As I was saying..."

"He's visiting, too? At your home?" Her tone was well past insinuating.

He glanced at her involuntarily. "Well, yes," he said, half-apologetic without meaning to be. "He called a couple of days ago and sort of invited himself. I didn't think you'd mind."

"No. I don't mind," she said slowly, obviously lying. Then further, "Has Alex said... anything to you about me?"

"No," Dan replied, half-lying. He and Radford had never had that talk about her they were supposed to have.

"Oh." She relaxed. "Well, where are we going tonight?"

She patted his hand again as it rested on the gearshift. Dan exited the highway and headed into town.

"A place called Huckleberry's," he said glad to be back making small talk.

"What's it like?" Evelyn found herself glad for small talk also.

"It used to be a college hangout, but now it's pretentious after its own fashion. The décor is supposed to suggest Mark Twain's world–riverboats and all that–the menu is supposed to have Cajun influence, but it's really just steaks and seafood."

This, he realized suddenly, was the way. Keep things light, superficial. Soon they would be at Grandfather's; from then until she left it would simply be a matter of keeping everyone together as much as possible. He was not certain how he would handle her if she wanted to sleep with him. Ramona's comment about men and their glands came back to him in a rush, and he felt a little ashamed. He made a silent vow to be faithful to Audrey.

They reached his street and he turned onto. The familiar houses spilled warm light into the freezing dusk. He turned left as he had done a thousand times before and drove around behind the house.

"You must meet Maisie first," he said as he got her luggage from the car's trunk. "She's our housekeeper. She's been with the family as long as I have."

They went into the house through the back door. As they entered the kitchen, Maisie hurried to them wiping her hands on a towel.

"Hello, I'm Maisie," she said forthrightly to Evelyn.

Evelyn seemed a bit confused, but she took Maisie's proffered hand and greeted her warmly.

As they made their way down the hall toward Grandfather Deal's study a few minutes later, Dan asked, "Why did you act surprised when you met Maisie?"

Evelyn smiled sheepishly. "Well, you're the great Southern gentleman…" she paused.

"And?"

Evelyn shrugged. "I… I thought she'd be black."

They stared at each other for a moment, then both burst out laughing.

XXXXII

They were still laughing when they went into the study.

Grandfather Deal sat watching the fire. The stereo wafted Chopin through the room. Dan took Evelyn's arm and led her over to the old man's chair.

"Grandfather," he said quietly, "this is Evelyn."

As Grandfather looked up, Evelyn neatly curtsied. Both he and Dan were surprised and charmed by the gesture.

"Well." He got slowly to his feet. "This is the young lady you felt strongly enough about to invite here for a visit."

"Yes sir," Dan replied uneasily. "This is she."

Evelyn stood quietly looking demure. She realized suddenly that winning the grandfather might win the grandson.

Grandfather Deal considered them both. They were so young. He smiled benevolently and said, "Daniel, take the young lady up to her room. She's probably tired and will want to freshen up before you young folks go out on the town."

"Yes sir."

Dan took Evelyn's arm again and tried to turn her toward the door. He suddenly felt a strong urge to get her away from his grandfather.

"Very nice to meet you, Mr. Deal," she said sweetly. "I look forward to talking with you soon."

"And I with you," replied Grandfather.

Dan hurried her out of the study and upstairs to her room. He dropped her bags onto the floor when they got there.

"You've got twenty-five minutes to get ready," he said brusquely.

He turned away to go to his own room, then turned back sharply. "Shall I ask Ramona to come to you?" he asked.

She studied his face. It occurred to her that he was probably more like Jason than Alex. His good manners were simply a coating.

"Yes, do," she said deliberately. "I'm looking forward to meeting her."

She turned from him and began assessing herself in the dresser mirror.

"Fine." Dan sensed that she was somehow ahead of him, but he was not sure how. "You may use the hall bathroom. I'll put out fresh towels for you. I'll go to Grandfather's room and use his private bath."

Without waiting for a response, Dan went across the hall to his own room. His clothes were already laid out for him. He supposed that was Ramona's doing. In spite of himself he smiled, pleased at her thoughtfulness to him, even with the house full of company.

He got his things together and set out for Grandfather's bathroom. As he passed Alex's room, through the half-opened door he caught a glimpse of Alex and Ramona standing by the window talking quietly.

He stepped into the room. "Alex, you look quite dignified. And Ramona, you are, as always, lovely."

They turned to him surprised, perhaps, he thought, looking slightly guilty.

Ramona collected herself first. "You look unready," she said. "We have to leave in twenty minutes to be on time."

"I'll be ready," he said offhandedly. Then he added confidentially, "Thanks for laying out my clothes, Ramona." He took note of the sudden look that passed between his cousin and his friend. Much had evidently been shared in the hour or so he'd been gone. He felt a twinge of jealousy.

"Oh, Ramona, could you go down to Evelyn's room?" he said sweetly. "She wants to meet you, and she might want some advice about dressing for this evening."

Ramona gave him an icy look, then made her way across the room, brushed by him and was gone.

"Dan," Alex began as soon as Ramona was out of earshot.

Dan held up his hand to stop him. "Sorry, Alex. Let me grab a shower and change. We can talk in the car on the way to Huckleberry's." He started for the door, then threw over his shoulder, "By the way, we can take your car, can't we? Mine only holds two, you know."

"Sure," Alex said, "But–"

"I won't be long." Dan hurried down the hall to his grandfather's room, leaving the pursuing Alex in the hallway as he closed the door.

XXXXIII

The meal was excellent, the service superb. After the second bottle of Beaujolais was finished and they'd ordered a bottle of champagne to be brought around just before midnight, they made their way to the lounge.

Ramona and Evelyn went to the women's room. Dan and Alex chose a table not too far from the dance floor, not too close to the band.

"Do you like dancing?" Dan asked Alex as they sat down.

"Pretty well. One must, for *les femmes*, it seems."

"You know," said Alex, "it's nice to go to a place that still has live music. So many clubs are going disco, now." He scanned the stage. "Have you seen these folks before? What sort of music do they play?"

Dan shrugged. "Once or twice. They play a mish mash. Some top forty. Some beach music. See the guy with the beard and the paunch? He used to teach in my high school."

Alex smiled. "The music business seems to agree with him."

"Indeed."

A pause.

"Oh, Alex," Dan began, "what were you wanting to talk with me about earlier this evening?"

The band launched into a song and it became nearly impossible to talk.

"Never mind," Alex shouted. "It'll keep another night. We'll talk tomorrow."

Just then Ramona and Evelyn rejoined them and asked them to dance. They took to the dance floor for nearly the entire forty-five minute set.

When the band took a break, they returned to their seats, exhilarated and exhausted. Alex ordered beer for everyone.

"Well," he said as he slumped in his chair, "that was lively enough."

"Actually–" Dan stopped, took the beer the waitress offered him, drew deeply on it. "I didn't originally plan for us to come here."

In response to their puzzled looks he added, "To the lounge, I mean."

The others looked even more puzzled.

"When I made the dinner reservations, I just planned on a nice dinner," he continued. "Then they offered this New Year's Eve package with admission to the lounge and a complimentary bottle of champagne for a *prix fixe*." Ramona rolled her eyes at his use of the French term. "And I thought you all would enjoy it, so...." He shrugged and smiled shyly.

"I'm having a great time," Evelyn said, leaning toward him and combing her hair with her fingers. "The dancing is fun. And the band is really good. Do you think they know 'We Can Work It Out' by the Beatles?"

"Probably," said Ramona. "They seem to know every other song from our child hoods," she added dryly.

Alex patted her hand. "I take it you'd prefer that their play list were more contemporary."

"Something like that." Ramona winked at him.

Dan looked at them surprised and displeased at the speed with which they had become familiar.

"Oh, Ramona, don't tell me you're a disco fan," said Evelyn. "We're struggling against it at Wake Forest."

"We've embraced it at William and Mary," Ramona replied cattily. "That way we don't have to pretend to be in love with someone if we just want to go to bed with him." She looked from Evelyn to Dan and back again.

Evelyn blushed, then reddened with anger. She looked at Ramona, then at Alex. She started to speak, but Alex made a gesture and she stopped.

Dan watched it all with first surprise, then vague recognition, then real dismay. He didn't understand it all, but he knew it concerned Alex and Evelyn and Ramona, and he guessed himself, too.

The band ended their break, so Alex asked Evelyn to dance. Once they were away from the table, he leaned toward Ramona.

"That was the cruelest I believe I've ever seen you behave," he said.

She sipped her beer and said nothing. He wasn't sure she'd heard him. "I said, that was the cruelest I've ever seen you behave."

Ramona looked disgustedly at him, then turned away to watch the dancing.

The band began a slow tune. Dan got up and went around to her. She took his proffered hand and they found their way into the sea of couples ebbing and flowing to the music.

They danced very close together. Ramona nuzzled her face into his neck. The song was, 'A Long, Long Time,' a Linda Ronstadt tune that had been popular when they were in high school; it was one they had first danced to in Ramona's room as she practiced for her first homecoming dance.

"Are you remembering?" Dan whispered.

"My freshman year in high school. You helped me practice my dancing before homecoming." She looked up at him and smiled, then laid her head on his shoulder again.

"Ramona?"

"Hmm?"

"Please don't be cruel to Evelyn. It's not necessary. She's no threat."

She trembled slightly to hear her own words given back to her. He gave her a light press on her back with his hand.

She looked up at him, drawing his eyes to hers. "Is that so, Dan?"

He nodded solemnly. "Yes."

The band segued from the slow song into a fast one, so they separated with no more words. Halfway through the song Alex and Evelyn danced up beside them. Alex indicated he wanted to change partners, so he and Dan stepped around each other and took their places opposite their dates.

They continued to dance for the rest of the set, another marathon. When they returned to their table, Alex gestured to the waitress.

"Four fresh beers and an oxygen tank," he said as she came up.

"Four beers," she said sullenly and walked away.

"Well, she was cheery," said Ramona, dryly.

"She has to work while everyone else has a party. I'm sure that isn't much fun," Evelyn said gently.

Dan and Alex looked at her in pleased surprise. Then they caught each other's eyes and looked away.

Evelyn sipped her beer. "Ugh. This is warm."

"You're right, Evelyn," Ramona offered tentatively. "I'm sure dealing with a crowd of drunks can get annoying."

She looked at Dan who gave her a fleeting smile of thanks. He knew she was trying to be agreeable.

Alex drew himself up haughtily. "Are you casting aspersions on my sobriety, ma'am?"

Ramona smiled sweetly, insinuatingly at him. "Sir, I cast no aspersions. I merely have made an observation. If from that you derive guilt, perhaps the guilt is justified."

Alex stood abruptly. "Ma'am, they have fired on Fort Sumter. Good evening to you."

He stalked away from the table.

Surprised by his action, Ramona watched uncertainly as he made his way toward the exit, then turned and went into the hallway leading to the men's room. He leaned back into sight, waved jauntily, and disappeared again.

"That Alex," said Evelyn. A wistful tenderness in her voice made both Ramona and Dan look at her as if she'd given away some secret.

"Do you mean 'that Alex' as in 'what a funny guy' or as in *what a weirdo*?" Ramona asked, hoping she sounded facetious and not curious.

Evelyn smiled, guiltily, Dan thought. A scene of a girl running down a hallway flashed through his mind. And Alex had always been cold to her.

"How do you...?" he began, sensing Evelyn knew Alex in a way he'd never imagined.

"I... I just meant his sense of humor is sort of... unusual." Evelyn picked up the fresh beer the waitress had just put before her and took a long drink.

Ramona, sensing some sort of crisis approaching, said cheerily, "He has a sprightly wit. No doubt about that."

She took a long drink of her own beer and waited to see if she'd done any good.

Dan looked at her, incredulous. "A sprightly wit?"

Ramona knew then that she'd successfully diverted his attention. "That's what I said," she replied archly. "What's wrong with that?" She raised her eyebrows.

"Well," he said, wondering where to go with the conversation, "you two sit here and discuss my friend behind his back as if..."

He groped momentarily. "As if he were some sort of...." He was at a loss. "Lab animal," he concluded lamely.

"Oh, no, not at all," Evelyn said, tossing her head. She was glad to respond to this silliness and avoid questions about herself and Alex. "We simply find Alex..." she fumbled, not wanting to say anything that might be taken as evidence. "Unique." She looked at Ramona and shrugged.

"His own man," added Ramona, knowing exactly which of Dan's buttons to push.

"Memorable," blurted Evelyn, her face reddening slightly.

"Downright remarkable." Ramona banged her fist lightly on the table.

Dan sat back in his chair and crossed his arms.

"Well," he said, sounding to Ramona remarkably like her Uncle Charles, "I don't find Alex unique, nor do I find him particularly *memorable*."

His look at Evelyn as he said the word *memorable* made her focus all her attention on her beer.

"He is," Dan continued, "an intelligent, well-spoken young man with a dry wit and a sense of humor much like my own."

He took up his beer and sipped it, waiting for their reply.

Ramona and Evelyn looked at each other. Then they shook their heads pityingly.

"Self satisfied?" said Ramona.

"Conceited. Definitely conceited." Evelyn pursed her lips and nodded her head sagely.

"Now, just a minute," Dan said, putting down his beer. "All I have done is correct your somewhat overwrought analysis of my friend's character. Now you have responded with an equally flippant consideration of my own."

"Oh, doesn't he sound just like a lawyer?" Ramona said in an exaggerated imitation of Vivian Leigh's Scarlet O'Hara.

"Surely he does," Evelyn added in a poor attempt at the same voice. "I surely want him..." She paused just long enough to be suggestive, then added, "on my side in court." She smiled at him saucily.

Alex returned to the table and took his seat.

"How are things with the war?" Dan asked, nodding toward the restrooms.

"It's too terrible to talk about in front of ladies," he said dramatically. "What went on while I was away?"

Dan leaned toward him confidentially. "I've been defending your honor, sir, against these honey-tongued critics."

Alex looked incredulous. "These fine ladies? I cannot believe it, sir."

"Believe it, sir," Dan said. He sighed and pushed back his chair. "And now you must defend yourself. I am off to the war. I have a patriotic duty."

Even across the room he could hear Evelyn's laughter as she talked to Alex. He wondered what was between them.

Then the music began and drowned it all out.

XXXXIV

When Dan got back to the table, the others were discussing leaving. He looked around at the bustle and noise. Dread of being alone with Evelyn clutched at him.

"Why do you all want to leave?" he asked poignantly to no one in particular.

Ramona reached over and took his hand. "Evelyn made a comment about how crowded this place had become, and I said wouldn't it be nice to be at home before a warm fire, and Alex said he had no objection if you were willing to go. What do you think?"

Dan looked at her expectant face. "It seems settled to me," he said wryly.

"Can we get our free champagne?" Alex asked.

Dan shrugged. "Well, we paid for it. It couldn't hurt to ask, I suppose."

He looked around the room until he caught the waitress's eye. When he requested the champagne, she offered no resistance.

"Seems okay with me," she said. "I'll have to check with the assistant manager, but you folks paid for dinner, and the champagne goes with that."

The assistant manger, however, complicated things.

First, he came to their table to ask if anything were wrong. When Alex tried to explain that all they wanted to do was see the New Year in on a quiet note, he offered to have the band play more softly.

When Dan intervened and tried to convince him that they'd had a wonderful time and simply wanted to leave, he ordered more beer for them.

Only when Ramona feigned a headache and tears did he give in and go get their champagne.

"Must be new in the job," Alex said when the overzealous one had gone.

"He certainly was solicitous." Dan shifted in his seat.

The assistant manger returned with two bottles of champagne.

"I thought we only got one bottle," Dan said.

193

"You each ordered dinner for two, didn't you?" He glanced back and forth between Dan and Alex.

"Yes." Alex shrugged.

"Then you each get a bottle of champagne. Compliments of Huckleberry's." He ceremoniously placed the bottles on the table. They were already in bags; only the foil covered corks showed. "We at Huckleberry's wish you all a good evening. And a Happy New Year." He bowed formally and was gone.

"Well, that finally worked out." Ramona began to slip her arms into the sleeves of her overcoat. Alex stood and helped her. Dan politely helped Evelyn.

They left money on the table to cover the cost of the beer and a generous tip, and made their way out. The parking lot was full and drivers were circling, looking for spaces. A red Camaro waited until Alex had backed out then moved into the space he'd vacated.

"It's kind of sad to be leaving now," Evelyn said as they pulled onto the highway. "The most exciting part is yet to come."

"I can't say I'm sorry," Dan said. "A cozy fire, good friends, and a glass of champagne will do me for the rest of this evening." He leaned against the car window and let his breath make fog against the chill glass.

"I wonder what sort of vintage champagne we've got?" Alex said. "Check the bottle, will you, Ramona?"

She pulled the champagne from its bag and held it up so that car lights from behind shone on its label. "It's bulk process California champagne," she read aloud.

"That means it's made in big copper vats and pumped full of bubbles," Alex said disparagingly. "I feared as much. Look under the seat."

Ramona reached under the car seat and pulled up a bottle sans bag.

Dan knew at once that it was Möet et Chandon. Not Dom Perignon, but a damned sight better than the swill they'd gotten at Huckleberry's.

He reached over the front seat and took the bottle of restaurant champagne. He rolled his window down and tossed it out. He saw the bottle bounce once on the shoulder of the road, then disappear into the ditch.

As he reached for his own bottle, Evelyn put her hand on top of it. "I'm saving this," she said, smiling at him in the darkness. "It might come in handy."

"I'd watch out if I were you," Alex said teasingly. "It might cause you to perform unnatural acts."

Ramona looked at him askance. He shrugged guiltily. "How do *you* happen to know that, Alex?" Her voice was low, thrilling.

"I read it... I read it in my high school health book. The chapter called, 'Things Cheap Wine Will Do to You.' " Ramona leaned over and whispered to him. He made a left turn.

She turned to Evelyn. "May I have some of that wine, Evelyn? Just because my date doesn't want to perform unnatural acts doesn't mean I don't want to."

The car swerved.

"Careful, there," Dan said, suddenly very uncomfortable.

They turned onto Dan's street. Alex drove around to the back of the house. Maisie had kindly left on the light for them.

They went in through the laundry room. Evelyn and Ramona stayed in the kitchen. They fixed a plate of fruit and cheese and got champagne glasses.

Dan and Alex went to the study and punched the nearly dead fire back to life. They had it blazing merrily when Ramona and Evelyn arrived.

Evelyn put the tray on the hearth before the fire. Ramona took a match from the mantle and lit a pair of candles they'd brought in from the dining room, then turned out all the lights except for a reading lamp on Grandfather Deal's desk across the room from the fireplace.

"Ah, very romantic," Alex said, stretching out before the fire. He picked up the bottle of Möet et Chandon he'd brought in. "Le champagne, monsieur." He held out the bottle to Dan.

Instead of taking the proffered bottle, Dan picked up his bottle of restaurant champagne. "Let's have this first," he said. "We'll appreciate the good wine more that way."

"We should put this on ice, then. It'll get warm by the time we get that swill down," Alex replied.

He got to his feet. "Ramona, could we get some ice for this?" He gestured with the bottle he held.

"Follow me." Ramona led him away to the kitchen.

Evelyn took a seat on the floor near the fire. She patted the floor beside her. "Sit down and talk with me, Dan."

He sat down beside her and showed her the champagne. "You can always tell a good champagne by the quality of the plastic used in the pseudo cork."

She laughed softly and drew her knees up to her chest. She rested her chin on them. "Dan, do you still have feelings for me?"

Dan pulled the wire wrapper from around the plastic cork and began working it out. It exploded from the bottle and landed in the fireplace behind the burning logs. "Well." Dan shrugged. "Looks as if we'll have to drink the whole bottle."

"Shouldn't we get that plastic thing out of the fire? If it melts, won't it give off toxic fumes or something?" She craned her neck trying to see the cork.

"You're probably right." Dan got up and picked up the poker. He raked about in the ashes and retrieved the plastic cork, filthy but undamaged.

"There. No danger now," he said briskly.

Evelyn had poured two glasses of the wine. She handed one to Dan as he sat down. "You didn't answer my question," she said as he sat down.

"I got the cork out of the fire. As for fumes, I don't know. You're probably right." He drank down his wine in greedy swallows. It was acidic and bitter. He poured himself another glass.

"My first question." She put down her glass and hugged her knees.

"We have returned." Alex marched into the room carrying the champagne in an ice bucket as if it were a sacred relic.

The bottle was open. Ramona followed, carrying two glasses and giggling.

Alex carefully placed the bucket on the hearth by the tray. He stepped back and genuflected. He took a seat on the floor.

Ramona came up beside him, crossed her ankles, and settled gracefully beside him like a flower landing in a pool of water.

"Not badly done, if I do say so," Alex said, reaching over and patting the bottle. "When I served as an acolyte at St. Phillip's, I was so steady they used to have me carry the New Testament during progressive readings."

"You're a credit to acolytes everywhere," Dan said. Then added, wryly, "I see you've already sampled the Möet."

"An accident," Alex said, his right hand raised, his left held against his chest so that he appeared supplicating. "As Ramona prepared the ice bucket, the cork leapt out of the bottle and into my hand. But don't worry." He reached over to pat Dan's shoulder and almost toppled both bottles of wine.

"Steady there, brave acolyte." Dan grabbed both bottles. Ramona helped Alex regain his balance.

"Sorry." He nodded to each of them in turn.

"Just so you saved us some of the good wine." Evelyn took a piece of cheese from the tray and nibbled it.

"There's enough for everyone to have a glass at midnight," Ramona said. "By the way, what time is it?"

Squinting in the firelight, Dan checked his watch. "Eleven-fifty. For the next ten minutes we can drink." He picked up the restaurant champagne. "This stuff. Better yet, for the next ten minutes we can drink nothing."

Alex took the bottle from Dan and poured some wine into a glass. "The thought of no wine is worse than the thought of bad wine." He put down the bottle and picked up his newly filled glass. "Cheers, all."

Evelyn replaced her untouched glass of wine on the tray.

Ramona shook her head but said nothing.

Dan finished his glass of wine, made a face at its taste, and put down his glass.

After he'd finished his own glass of wine, Alex added his to those on the tray.

The group sat and stared into the fire, each thinking his or her private thoughts.

After several minutes, Alex took charge of the fire, poking the half-burned logs into a brighter flame and adding a small log. When he returned to his seat, the meditations resumed.

"Are we meditating on what the old year hath wrought or pondering what the New Year may bring?" Ramona asked wryly to break the spell.

"As for myself, I feel rather indifferent about both. What about you, Alex?"

Alex continued to stare at the fire, as did Evelyn. Dan seemed to be the only one to have heard her.

"The New Year should bring optimism," he said quietly.

"I'm sure for some it does," she replied. "One's prospects color one's outlook, n'est-ce pas?"

"Vraiment," Evelyn murmured.

Both she and Alex had returned from their reveries.

"What time is it, Dan?" Alex asked briskly, taking up the Moet and pouring wine into glasses.

He tossed the restaurant champagne in Evelyn's glass into the fire where it blazed up like gasoline. He and Dan looked first at each other, then at their stomachs. Everyone laughed.

"Time?" Alex asked.

Dan checked his watch. "Uh oh. Three past twelve, we missed the big moment." He yawned. "Excuse me. Too much fine wine."

Everyone laughed again.

Alex handed around the glasses. "The New Year is still very young. I intend to drink a toast to its possibilities."

He smiled at Ramona and she smiled in return. Their smiles made Dan uneasy.

Then, suddenly solemn, the group touched glasses.

"Happy New Year," Evelyn whispered.

"Happy New Year," Dan replied gently. They touched glasses again and drank their wine.

As he took his glass from his mouth, Dan noticed that Ramona and Alex were kissing. He felt a twinge of jealousy.

He turned to Evelyn. She leaned toward him and they kissed.

As they parted Dan saw that Alex and Ramona were still kissing. "Don't you people need to breathe?" he asked, only partly in jest.

They broke apart. Ramona brushed her hair back on one side. "Don't spoil a good time, Dan," she said dryly.

Alex said nothing. Even in the firelight it was clear he was blushing.

"Cat got your tongue, Alex?" Ramona said softly, brushing back a lock of his hair with her fingertips.

"Maybe you bit it off," Evelyn blurted.

Everyone looked at her. She hung her head. No one spoke for several moments.

Alex took Ramona's hand and kissed it. "Thank you," he said quietly.

Dan was struck by the sincerity of the gesture.

As if aware that Dan was watching them, Alex suddenly stretched and yawned. "Excuse me," he said facetiously. "It's getting past my bedtime."

"Is that so?" Ramona's voice was insinuating.

Dan felt goose bumps rise on his arms.

"If you haven't succeeded by midnight, do you give up?" she continued, putting her hand on Alex's knee.

Alex looked from Ramona to Evelyn almost guiltily it seemed to Dan. "How did we get mixed up with such wanton creatures, Daniel?" he asked.

"Well, this one." He gestured at Ramona. "Was born into my family... And this one." He turned to Evelyn and she smiled shyly. "Came to me in the night as I read Yeats."

"Nicely put," said Alex.

"Speak for yourself." Ramona clasped her hair in one hand, pulled it back then shook it free. "The same thing *he* said about *me* being born into *his* family might be said about *him* being born into *mine*."

"I was talking about Dan's description of how Evelyn came into his life. It was poetic... and gentlemanly." He wrinkled his nose at Ramona who did the same back at him.

"Why are you two obsessed with being gentlemen?" Evelyn asked Alex, her voice soft, dramatic.

"We're not obsessed. We're simply gentlemen," Dan said quietly.

"And what, Daniel Randolph Deal, soon to be Esquire, is a gentleman?" Ramona asked.

Dan considered.

"A gentleman..." he began, then realized he had no answer.

Evelyn touched him on the sleeve. Suddenly, he felt sure of himself.

"A gentleman," he said slowly, "is one who answers all questions and requests graciously, even those that might be facetious, or of ill intent."

Alex nodded, making a satisfied face as he did so. "Again, nicely put."

Evelyn gave Dan's arm a squeeze, then stifled a yawn. She brightened suddenly and said, "We should have a slumber party."

Dan looked incredulous.

Alex smiled and shrugged. "Well, Dan, as you said, a gentleman is gracious to all questions and requests."

"Nicely put." Ramona put her tongue in her cheek exaggeratedly and pointed at it.

Everyone laughed.

Dan turned to Evelyn. "We are at your service, ma'am. How should we proceed?"

Ramona got to her feet. "We should all go upstairs and put on our pajamas. Then we'll make some hot chocolate."

Ramona went to Evelyn and helped her up. "Come on. We'll change quickly, then we'll pamper these gentlemen and make the hot chocolate." They marched briskly from the room.

Dan stayed behind and stoked up the fire. Alex gathered the remains of the champagne and snacks and carried them to the kitchen. Dan waited for him in the hallway, and they went upstairs together.

XXXXV

Dan went to his room and quickly changed in the dark. It was cold in his room and very still. His movements seemed a violation of the place's peace, so he hurried.

Once dressed, he slipped from the room and made his way down the hall. Evelyn's and Ramona's rooms were dark; they had evidently been as good as their words and were already downstairs.

As he passed Alex's room, the light was still on and the door was ajar. He went in. Alex stood by the bed in pajamas and a robe. He had on a pair of dark socks.

"Haven't got an extra pair of slippers have you, Dan?" Alex looked down at his stocking feet and wiggled his toes. "This looks silly. And it's too damned cold to go barefoot."

Dan smiled. "No. But I suspect Grandfather does. He gets a couple of new pair every Christmas. Let me slip into his room and check."

He made his way to his grandfather's room. He stopped at the door and listened. Silence. The doorknob turned easily and he opened the door just enough to let himself in.

Grandfather Deal's nightlight cast "a little glooming light", as Spenser would say. As he made his way around his grandfather's bed, Dan stubbed his toe on the corner of a blanket chest at the foot of the bed. He bit his finger to stifle a yelp.

At the bedside he looked down at the old gentleman. Grandfather Deal's white hair shone silvery in the dim light, his features relaxed in an expression neither happy nor sad, merely at peace. The sleep of the just, Dan thought.

The closet door creaked when Dan tried it. Grandfather rumbled in his bed and Dan froze, half expecting the old man's head to rise from the bed and address him in a hoarse whisper, but that didn't happen.

Dan closed the door behind him and felt for the light switch. When he harsh incandescence flashed on, he saw a half dozen pairs of slippers nestled on a shoe rack at his feet. He took a pair that Ramona had given his grandfather the previous Christmas and that he had complained were too large.

He oriented himself to the door and clicked off the light. When he slipped out, the closet door didn't creak.

As he passed the bed he looked back at his grandfather again. The old man's eyes opened and he turned his head toward Dan.

"Stuart?" he whispered.

"Sir?" In spite of himself, Dan answered automatically.

"Stuart? Is that you, son?"

Dan realized then that the old man was dreaming, that he thought he was talking to Dan's father, his oldest son. He didn't know what else to do so he answered. "Yes sir. It's me... Stuart."

"Be careful, son." Grandfather turned away then, but Dan heard him say, rather indistinctly, "Be very careful."

Dan involuntarily shivered as he left the room. He was still musing over the experience when he got to Alex's room and handed him the slippers.

"You took your time," Alex said as he took the shoes. Then he noticed Dan's expression. "Something happen?"

Dan related the incident to him.

"I guess that was weird," Alex said thoughtfully. Then, without considering, he asked, "How long has your dad been dead, Dan?"

He immediately apologized and retracted his question, but Dan waved his hand casually to show he'd taken no offense.

"Nineteen years come this May," he said. "I was only four when he died."

"And your mother married a Frenchman?" Alex's tone betrayed a true Southerner's disbelief that a woman of the South could be attracted to anyone except a man of the South.

"Asked in the same tone my grandfather would have taken," Dan replied, laughing. "Yes, she married a Frenchman. She's lived in France for about fifteen years. I visited her a couple of years ago. Shall we go down?"

Alex would have liked to ask more questions. He liked Dan and wanted to know him better.

Dan would have liked him to ask. He wanted Alex to know him better.

Unfortunately, Alex took Dan's invitation to go downstairs to mean that he wished to end the conversation.

Dan, on the other hand, was realizing that Alex was really his friend. He would have liked to unburden himself of the whole mess: Evelyn, Audrey, and Alicia. He made a mental note to try to get away with Alex at some point during the weekend and discuss things with him.

As it turned out, they got to be alone sooner than Dan expected. When Alex and Dan got down to the study, Evelyn and Ramona were asleep, curled up before the fire like two cats.

Dan got Afghans from the sofa and from Grandfather Deal's chair. One he gave to Alex for Ramona; the other he spread over Evelyn.

"Looks like there'll be no hot chocolate," Alex said. "I was sort of hoping for some myself." He took up the poker and gingerly prodded the fire trying not to disturb the sleepers.

"We could make some ourselves," Dan offered. "I have another idea, though." He went to a cabinet against the far wall and got a bottle of brandy and two snifters. He brought them over and set them on the hearth to warm. "This will be better than cocoa," he said.

Alex sat down on the hearth. "I've always wanted to do this," he said quietly.

"Have a slumber party?" Dan sat down also and felt the brandy bottle. "How warm is this stuff supposed to get?"

"Hmm. Which question shall I answer first?" Alex asked. He smiled. "What I meant was I've always wanted to sit around with some other chap and have a brandy before a blazing fire. Seems so British and right, you know?"

Dan nodded.

"As for the second question, I have no idea how warm brandy is supposed to get."

"Ah. Well, I say it's warm enough." Dan uncapped the brandy and poured some into each glass. He handed a snifter to Alex who swirled his drink and watched it, fascinated.

Suddenly he looked at Dan and grinned sheepishly. "I've always wanted to do that, too." He held up his glass in a toast. "Cheers."

Dan did likewise. "To the sleeping beauties," he said. They touched glasses and drank. The brandy made a smooth burning track down their throats.

Alex held his glass away from him and eyed it with suspicion. "I've drunk too much tonight," he said, more to himself than to Dan.

He put his glass on the hearth. "Dan," he said his tone serious, "I need to talk with you about something. Would you mind?"

"Not at all, Alex. We can continue the conversation we began upstairs." Dan turned up his glass and drained it. The liquor made his eyes water. He poured himself another drink while waiting for Alex to lead the conversation. Alex said nothing.

Dan drank his next glass of brandy more slowly, stopping between swallows to watch the brown liquid swirl in the bottom of his glass. He finished it and put his glass down slowly. He realized suddenly that he was quite drunk.

"Alex, are we friends?" he asked. His speech felt thick, like molasses.

Alex, who had been preoccupied with his own thoughts about how to tell Dan of his relationship with Evelyn, started. When he turned to Dan he realized that the brandy was having a powerful effect on his friend. "Of course, Dan. We've become close friends."

Dan leaned forward and put his face in his hands. "Forgive me, Alex. I'm drunk."

Alex put his arm around Dan's shoulder. "You're all right, Dan Deal," he said, laughing.

Evelyn stirred and Alex stood suddenly. The brandy made him feel slightly light-headed, so he sat down again. Evelyn was only moving in her sleep.

"Dan," he said, still watching her, "we have to talk about Evelyn."

"She's one of several we have to talk about."

Dan shook his head to try and clear it and turned to Alex. Alex's face blurred and he blinked several times.

"Alex," he slurred, "let me put this legalistically. Is there now, or has there ever been, a 'special woman' in your life?"

Alex looked at the sleeping Evelyn. "In the past, yes. At present..." he glanced at Ramona, said, "no. In the future—" then turned to Dan as if to ask a question. "One has hopes."

"Ramona likes you, Alex. Very much."

After he'd said it, Dan wasn't sure he wanted it to be true.

He looked at his cousin. It seemed to him that she would accept whatever role he prescribed for her. He had a momentary vision of Ramona and Alex together. The thought, or something else, brought on a slight wave of nausea. He was suddenly far too warm.

He got unsteadily to his feet. "Let's go sit on the sofa, Alex."

When his friend didn't immediately respond, Dan held out his hand to him. "Come, Alex. It'll be cooler over there. Don't you find it too warm here by the fire?"

Alex took hold of his hand and tugged gently. Dan sat down hard on the stone hearth. The room swam.

"Dan, you were swaying like a reed in a breeze." Alex leaned toward him. "You look a little queasy, Dan. Do you think you might be sick?"

Moving his hand slowly and carefully, Dan signaled no. He went forward onto his hands and knees and crawled past the sleepers to his grandfather's desk. He got the waste can from beside it and put it between his legs as he leaned back against the desk. When he turned his face to one side, the wood was cool to his skin and he felt better. Something moved suddenly across the room and he turned his head to see what it was. The room swam again. In spite of his efforts, he couldn't hold back the wave of nausea and he vomited into the waste can.

XXXXVI

There was a cool cloth on his forehead. His head was pillowed on Evelyn's breast. He turned his head slightly to one side; the scent of her perfume seemed overpowering. Another wave of nausea came.

He sat up, looking around for the waste can. The wet cloth unfolded partially and fell down over his nose. The cool, wet smell was soothing, and the nausea passed.

"What happened?" he croaked.

"Brandy on champagne on beer on Beaujolais," Alex said. He held out a glass of what appeared to be tomato juice. "Try some of this, " he said. "It works for me."

Dan took the glass in a slightly shaky hand and eyed it dubiously. "Is this one of those concoctions? With Tabasco sauce and raw eggs and all that sort of rot in it?"

Alex smiled. "No. Just tomato juice." He gestured at the glass. "Try it."

Dan sipped tentatively. It wasn't as bad as he'd expected; a couple of more sips and he felt like looking at everyone.

Alex sat across from him, calm and reassuring. Ramona was to Alex's right. She seemed to reach for and draw back from him in the same gesture, her face concerned, nervous. Evelyn, to his left, drew her fingers up and down his spine and looked at him benignly.

He put the glass of juice down carefully. His head was beginning to hurt. "This isn't like me," he said to no one in particular.

"We know." Evelyn's voice was husky.

"Do you feel so terrible?" asked Ramona softly. Dan tried to smile at her, but a sharp pain shot through his head over his right eye and he grimaced instead. "I guess you do," she said.

Dan picked up his juice and sipped a bit more, then asked, feeling very foolish as he did so, what had happened.

Alex told him that he'd crawled over to the desk, which Dan faintly remembered. Alex had been keeping an eye one him but had drowsed momentarily only to be awakened by the sound of

207

Dan's retching. Dan had passed out, his head hanging over the edge of the waste can by the time Alex had roused himself and gone over to offer aid.

He'd been working with Dan a couple of minutes when Evelyn and Ramona, awakened by the commotion, had come over to see what was wrong. They'd applied the cold cloth, cleaned up the waste can, and Evelyn had held him until he'd come around.

"How long was I out?" Dan asked.

Alex glanced at the clock over the fireplace. "Maybe ten minutes. Maybe fifteen." He looked around at the group. "The fire's dead. I suggest we go up to bed. You'll feel better there, Dan and the rest of us can get some real sleep." He went over to the fireplace and closed it up.

Dan tried to get to his feet but found himself unsteady.

"Give me your juice," Ramona said. She put the glass on the desk and then, with Evelyn's aid, helped Dan to his feet.

Once standing, Dan felt better. He took his arms from about the women's shoulders and made his way slowly across the room. At the door Alex offered to help him, but Dan declined.

They made their way upstairs. When they got to Alex's room, Ramona went in. Dan called weakly to her and she came to the door.

"Do you think this is a good idea?" He gestured at Alex, then at her.

Ramona looked at Alex. "It's what I want to do." She turned back to Dan. "We'll probably just talk," she said.

Dan shrugged wearily. "Remember what you told me about glands, dear. You can't build a relationship on sex. Believe me, I know."

The rueful note in his voice made Evelyn eye him askance. She narrowed her eyes, then, with effort, smiled.

"Dan, this is what I want right now," Ramona said.

"What about in the morning?" Alex asked.

She held out her hand to him and smiled. To Dan it was a smile like Evelyn's. "In the morning, we'll see."

Alex took her hand and she led him into the room and gently closed the door.

Evelyn took Dan's arm and they walked down the hall to their rooms. Evelyn quietly went to her door. Dan opened his and a rush of cold air made his head throb. "Could you get me some aspirin?" he asked without looking at her.

Shivering occasionally, he waited in the doorway while she fetched the aspirin. They seemed to expand to the size of marshmallows when he tried to put them into his mouth, and he sputtered and coughed as he tried to wash them down with the water she'd brought. While Evelyn returned the glass to the bathroom, Dan went in and got into bed.

Evelyn came to his door and peeked in. "Do you need anything else?"

"Yes."

"What?"

"You in here with me."

She came in and closed the door softly behind her. Once she was settled, Dan turned to her and laid his head against her breast. He felt no desire and was content to lie still as she stroked his hair. "That feels good," he said, his voice half-muffled.

"Dan?"

"Yes?"

"Would you like to make love?"

He raised himself on one elbow and looked at her face. The light from a street lamp left her in half silhouette. She smiled, creating an eerie visage that made Dan shudder. She pulled him to her and kissed him.

Embarrassed, he pulled away. "Isn't my breath horrible?" he asked.

"Oh, Dan," she said, sighing. "You know, the French don't care about such things."

He turned onto his back beside her. "The French don't care about many things," he said coolly.

She sighed again. "Why do you say that about the French, Dan?"

"The lessons of history teach it. My personal experience emphasizes it. My estimation of the character of the French people seems sound to me." Dan watched the movement of shadows thrown by tree branches dart across the ceiling. He realized he felt much better.

"What do you mean by 'personal experience'? Did some French girl break your heart while you were visiting your mother?" Evelyn asked playfully.

For some reason her tone infuriated him. "Not quite," he answered shortly.

He did not like the turn the conversation had taken. He did not want to tell her that his stepfather had introduced him to his mistress. "It's nothing that would interest you," he said flatly.

"Anything that concerns you interests me," she said tenderly. Her hand touched his shoulder before moving down his chest.

"I do not want to have sex with you, Evelyn," Dan said in a tone that one might use to explain something to a heedless child.

She drew her hand away and stiffened beside him. "Oh. I guess it's not all right to touch you now?" Her voice had a steely quality that Dan had never heard before in any woman's voice. "You didn't seem to mind my touch before *Audrey* came on the scene."

"*Audrey* is not the subject of this discussion. You will leave her out of this," Dan said as arrogantly as he'd ever said anything in his life.

Evelyn reared up onto her knees and looked down at him.

"Audrey most certainly *is* the subject of this conversation, Daniel. She's here in this bed right now. You're not refusing my offer of love because you feel sick. You're refusing me because of Audrey. I never asked for love, Dan. You're the one who insisted that everything be so romantic, that we play at falling in bve so you could rationalize your lust. And now you're playing at falling in love with her because you've had me as much as you want for now and she's the obscure object of your desire."

"As for me—" She stopped and smiled, rather wicked looking in the crazy light coming from the street lamps below. "I don't have to justify my lust. I just enjoy it when it comes."

She left the bed and went to the door.

Dan sat up. Pain throbbed over his right eye again, and he leaned forward holding his head in his hands. He thought that perhaps she would come back to him. Instead he hear the door click open and saw a flash of light from the hallway.

"Where are you going?" he asked in an overloud whisper.

"To my room," she said softly, saucily. "If you want to come over there, we'll screw. If not, stay here and sleep off your gentleman's drunk. Come or don't come. It's up to you."

She whirled out of the room leaving Dan, in spite of his headache, puzzling over her word choice.

XXXXVII

Dan did not go to her room. He had always found ultimatums offensive to both his sense and sensibility. An ultimatum of the style and substance of Evelyn's offended him far too much to allow him to consider acquiescing to it.

He wasn't sure when he finally fell asleep. He woke to a bright, cold room shot through with shafts of sunlight. He still wore his watch, so he squinted at it: 9:00 A.M. He felt terrible. He'd slept in his robe; he merely threw off the covers and got to his feet, an act that made his head throb for some moments. He walked gingerly to the door of his room and opened it.

Evelyn's door stood open. He crept across the hall and peeked in. The room was empty, the bed neatly made. Something about the room's appearance made Dan think that Evelyn was gone. He went in and got some clothes together, then went to shower and made himself presentable. Any crisis that might be occurring downstairs–and he felt strongly that one of some kind was–would have to wait.

XXXXVIII

Alex was sitting on his bed when Dan got back to his room. "Evelyn's downstairs with her bags," he said as Dan came in.

"I guessed she'd done something of that sort when I went into her room earlier. Has she said anything to you or Ramona?"

"Only that she was going home." He made room on the bed and Dan sat down beside him to put on socks and shoes. "Oh," he added, "she's also having a talk with your grandfather."

"Wonderful." Dan bent to tie his shoelace but looked instead at Alex. "Any idea what their talk was about?"

"No idea. She asked to see him behind closed doors."

Dan sighed. "Oh, god. I can imagine what she's saying to him." He tied his shoelaces, then stood.

Alex remained seated. "What was the fight about, Dan?"

Dan pulled on a sweater and adjusted his shirt collar. "Several things. The French. Personal hygiene. Let's see...."

Alex smiled wryly.

Dan continued. "It's complicated, as I suppose such matters are when one tries to explain them. Mostly, though, I'd say the fight was about Audrey."

Alex stood and patted Dan on the shoulder. "A bit of advice from a reformed rake, Daniel. You should never take two women to bed unless both are physically present."

Dan smiled sheepishly. "Evelyn has already made that clear to me."

Alex laughed softly. "Well, then."

They made their way from the room and down the hall to the stairs. Alex clapped Dan on the back as they started down. "Remember the word of the poet, Daniel: Excelsior!"

XXXXIX

Looking stern, Grandfather Deal stood with his back to the fireplace in the study. Evelyn stood a few feet away.

Dan had left Alex and Ramona waiting in the hall outside. Ramona was unabashedly eavesdropping; she had heard only enough to make her anxious. Alex was the picture of calm.

Dan closed the heavy oak door of the study and walked across the room to them.

"Good morning, Grandfather," he said politely.

He gave Evelyn a curt nod.

"Daniel," Grandfather Deal began, his voice reflecting anger, concern, and indecision. "Daniel, this young lady has cast some serious aspersions upon your character, and your honor. She claims—" He hesitated. "Asserts that you lied to her and..." There was another, longer hesitation. "Seduced her."

Dan was visibly startled. He was surprised at his grandfather's being able to say such a thing aloud, much less in the presence of a woman.

Dan turned to Evelyn and looked at her with unabashed disgust. He felt a mixture of embarrassment for himself, shame before his grandfather, and anger at Evelyn. He suddenly wondered how he could have cared for someone who would stoop to such a slatternly trick.

Evelyn glared back at him, an unrepentant fury.

It was then that he knew what he must do. He turned to his grandfather and looked him straight in the eye. "She's lying," he said quietly.

"I am not!" Evelyn fairly shouted.

Without looking at her, Dan said patronizingly, 'Hush. I am talking to Grandfather."

Evelyn moved to his side. She whispered into his ear, her words almost a hiss, *"Yes. You* are talking to *Grandfather.* I'm sure *you'll* be able to convince him that *I'm* lying, that *I'm* just some whore, that *you're* a *gentleman* who made a mistake, got caught in some passing fancy."

With some effort, Dan kept his temper.

"Evelyn, I intend to do no such thing," he said, keeping his eyes on his Grandfather's. "I will answer Grandfather's questions honestly. You will hear the entire conversation."

"And now." He turned to her with a look that made her draw back. "Move away from me, *please*." The last word sounded like a warning.

Dan turned back to his grandfather. "What, *exactly*, has Evelyn told you, sir?"

Grandfather Deal, evidently taken aback by the virulence of the exchange between Dan and Evelyn, didn't speak for over a minute.

"She says, Daniel," he said finally, "that you told her you loved her so she would–" He stopped, his sense of delicacy causing him to waver.

"Sleep with me?" Dan looked at Evelyn so hard that she took another step back from him.

"Yes." His grandfather's face was full of strange new looks that Dan had never seen before.

"She's lying," Dan said firmly.

Grandfather waited several moments for Dan to continue. When he didn't, Grandfather asked, "Well, son? Is that all?"

Dan nodded militarily. "That is all I have to say, sir. I am a gentleman. I have never lied to you, sir, or to her. I am a grown man and I owe no one any explanation. Whatever may have happened between us was consented to on her part without any duplicity, or duress, from me. If you choose to believe her—" he flashed a look of disgust at Evelyn, then turned back to his grandfather with a look of respectful determination— "you may."

He turned again to Evelyn, this time with a look of parental authority. "Are you packed and ready to leave?" he asked.

She nodded, too surprised to speak. Or so Dan assumed.

"Good," Dan said firmly. "I will take you back to your car. Then you may go home."

He went to the door, but as he reached it, he realized that Evelyn had not moved. "Now," he said, perhaps too loudly.

Evelyn went instead to Grandfather Deal. "Aren't you going to do anything?" she asked, her voice rising with each word. "He's doing just what I said he'd do. He's passing me off as some... some tramp," she said after groping for a word. "I...."
She stopped suddenly and visibly tried to calm herself. " Mr.

Deal," she said earnestly, "I... I love Dan. I really do. He didn't do anything." Her composure broke and she bent her head, sobbing.

Grandfather Deal started to reach for her, then abruptly turned his back to her.

His action surprised even Dan. He went to her and put his arm gently around her shoulders. She buried her face in his sweater.

"Grandfather, I'm going to take Evelyn to her car so she can go home," he said.

Grandfather Deal did not turn around. "Very well," he replied his voice formal. "Goodbye, Miss Daiches. I wish you well."

Then he did something that Dan considered ludicrous. He turned to Evelyn and said gently, "I am sorry if I have offended you."

Evelyn raised her head and looked at him. 'Mr.. Deal, I'm sorry, too."

Once she'd gotten that out, she wiped her eyes and looked at Dan. Her face was so soft and so sad that he felt a twinge of guilt.

"Let's go," he said gently, leading her away. When he closed the library door, Grandfather had returned to staring at the fireplace.

L

Alex and Ramona helped Dan put Evelyn's bags into the car.

"Goodbye, Evelyn," said Alex graciously as she sat stonily in the passenger seat. "Perhaps we'll see each other at Wake Forest."

She didn't answer.

He turned to Dan and shrugged. Ramona took his arm and they turned for the house.

Abruptly, Ramona came back and walked around to Evelyn's side of the car. She tapped on the car window. Evelyn didn't respond. She tapped again. Evelyn lowered the window slowly.

"Goodbye, Evelyn," Ramona said. "I'm sorry."

Evelyn turned to her and they looked at each other for a long minute. Then, looking straight ahead, Evelyn raised her window.

Ramona went back to Alex. Arm in arm they went into the house.

Dan turned the car around. As they drove slowly around the house, Dan saw his grandfather at a window in the seldom-used parlor. Dan waved. Grandfather nodded solemnly.

They reached the street, Dan turned right, and they were on their way.

Dan anticipated a long, silent drive.

Evelyn began talking before they reached the end of the street. She kept up a long, frivolous monologue about spring semester.

"I'm in the S.O.P.H. society, you know, Dan. We always have big dances in the spring. This year we're inviting the guys in Lambda Chi Alpha. Jason's an old Lambda Chi Alpha, you know."

At the mention of Manetti's name Dan frowned, but Evelyn either took no notice of his reaction or kept talking merely to annoy him.

"Jason takes part in the fraternity's activities as an old brother sometimes. I suppose he'll be my date for the dance. I guess I'll give him a call tonight."

She paused, waiting perhaps for some response from Dan. None came forth, so she continued.

"Oh, Dan, did I tell you? I'm going to France again. We leave February third. Six weeks in Dijon."

No reply.

"Where does your mother live, Dan? Maybe I could see her. Tell her hello from you."

She became quiet then. After a few moments Dan thought he heard her sniffle as if she were quietly crying. The thought gave Dan some small satisfaction.

"She lives in Nevers," he said, smiling to himself, "Nevers, en France."

"*Hiroshima, Mon Amour.*" They looked at each other for the first time then, even though the drive was nearly over.

"You know the film?" Dan said slowly, surprised.

Evelyn shrugged. "I've seen it. We had to read the screenplay for a course in contemporary French lit. Marguerite Duras. Who are we, what are we, and like that."

"Henri Bergson," Dan said. "We are all in a state of becoming what we will ultimately be."

Her eyes fixed on the side of Dan's face as he drove. "What are you becoming, Dan?" she asked, all seriousness.

Dan thought. It would be all too easy to be flippant. He could say he was becoming a lawyer. He could say he was becoming concerned because they were low on fuel.

It seemed pointless to fend her off any more, given their situation, so he said quietly, "I am becoming aware of any number of things, Evelyn. But the truth, if I can answer you truthfully, is that I am becoming aware of my limitations. Especially concerning women."

"What are those limitations?" she asked, almost coyly.

"You, Evelyn, probably know them better than I," he replied with a half smile.

They reached the exit for the service station where Evelyn's car was. Dan drove slowly up the ramp. They waited at the egress for the highway as several cars went past.

"Alex said I might see him at Wake Forest, Dan," Evelyn said softly. "Might I see you?"

He looked at her. It seemed to him that Evelyn always looked her loveliest asking a question. "Only by the merest chance," he said, hoping he didn't sound too unkind.

She turned and looked out her window. Dan pulled out into the highway, then turned almost immediately into the service station. They did not speak as she unloaded her bags. She folded the tissue receipt as she came out of the station.

An attendant brought her car around and loaded her bags. "Belt's fixed and the tank's full, ma'am. She's ready to go," he said as he handed her the keys.

"Thank you," she said.

The attendant went into the station.

Dan and Evelyn faced each other across one of the concrete islands on which the gas pumps stood. At that moment both of them realized how stupid and embarrassing the situation was.

Evelyn held out her hand. "Goodbye, Dan Deal," she said formally.

They shook hands.

Her hand lingered in his. In a spontaneous gesture, he leaned toward her and brought it to his lips.

She jerked it away. "Oh, to hell with this."

She turned and got into her car, slamming the door violently.

After a moment, she got back out of the car and stood with one foot propped on the doorjamb. Just like a man, Dan thought.

"Hey," she called to Dan. "How far is it to Winston-Salem?"

Manetti. Dan shook his head. He had to give her credit. She didn't stay down long.

"Something over 100 miles. Do you need a map?"

In reply she went into the station. The attendant who'd brought her car around came back out with her. She was insisting, too loudly, that he show her the most direct route to Winston-Salem.

He did.

She thanked him profusely.

When he'd gone back inside, she got into her car and started it. She rolled down her window and called to Dan.

"*Au revoir*, monsieur."

"Not very likely," he called back dryly.

She laughed and drove away. He watched her until she disappeared down the exit ramp.

Only when he got back into his car to leave did he remember that he was almost out of gas. He pulled up to the pumps.

"Yes sir," said the attendant as he came out to the car wiping his hands with one of those slate blue paper towels endemic to all service stations.

"Fill it up, please."

As the attendant filled his car's tank, Dan realized that he felt completely well. He was also hungry. He'd had no breakfast.

"Anyplace to eat breakfast around here?" he said to the attendant as he got out of his car.

"Ham and sausage biscuits in the refrigerator inside," replied the attendant, nodding toward the building. "You can heat them up in the microwave oven. Coffee, too."

Dan went inside and bought a sausage biscuit and hot cocoa. It was then that he realized he didn't have his wallet. He ran outside and stopped the gas pump that the attendant had left running while he saw to another customer.

Dan reached into his car and took out his loose change cup. He went inside and paid for the biscuit and cocoa, then counted the rest of his change.

The gas bill was two dollars more than he had. There was nothing to do except to explain to the attendant. This he did.

"May I bring you the two dollars this afternoon?" he asked as he finished his tale.

"You from Roanoke?" the attendant asked, trying to sound casual.

"Lynchburg."

The man nodded sagely. He looked at Dan's clothes, then at the car. The Porsche convinced him that Dan was good for the money.

"Why don't I just send you a bill?" he asked generously.

"That'll be fine," Dan replied humbly.

The attendant got out a charge ticket. "All right, then. I'll need your name, address and phone number, sir."

"My name is Daniel Randolph Deal," Dan said forcefully.

The attendant looked up, rather impressed by the name, or so it seemed. He began to write laboriously.

"Gentleman," Dan added firmly.

LI

Dan went back to Lynchburg and had a talk with his grandfather. The old gentleman admitted that Evelyn had taken him by surprise, and that, in light of his recent talk with Dan, he wasn't sure there might not be some truth in her accusations about his grandson.

"Grandfather!" Dan exclaimed, genuinely hurt that the old man could believe that he would stoop to such tactics with a woman.

Grandfather Deal got up from his chair and went over to the fireplace where Dan stood. Looking at the fire rather than at his grandson, he said, "After our discussion the other day, I wasn't sure I knew you at all, Daniel. But when I saw how you conducted yourself in the face of that girl's behavior, I knew you were a gentleman."

He sighed, then turned to Dan. "Times have changed, son. People don't behave as they once did."

His sad face reminded Dan of a portrait of Robert E. Lee that he'd admired many times in one of his grandfather's books.

"Your sort of Southern gentleman is different than mine, sir," the old man said wistfully.

"Well, Grandfather," Dan replied lightly, "this is the 'New South,' you know."

"So they say," Grandfather Deal murmured, more to himself than to Dan. "But it seemed to me the South would always be the South."

LII

Ramona and Alex took Dan out for a late lunch. Before they went, Ramona tried phoning Audrey, but she didn't answer.

At lunch Ramona was very animated; she talked continuously about the things the four of them–Dan, Audrey, Alex, and she– might do that evening. She finally agitated herself so that she left the table to call Audrey again, just as the food arrived.

Alex and Dan sat in silence for a few minutes; neither eating even though Ramona had admonished them to begin without her as she'd left the table.

Finally, Alex ventured a comment. "From all that Ramona tells me, Audrey sounds like a wonderful person. She might be just right for you." He took a sip of iced tea.

"She charming," Dan said noncommittally.

"No doubt."

A pause.

"Dan," Alex said suddenly, "do you remember that I said we needed to talk? About Evelyn?"

Dan laughed softly. "I surely do. But something always prevented us, didn't it?" He took a sip of his own tea. "I guess it doesn't matter now, does it?" he added, a little ruefully.

"I guess not." Alex sighed as if to relax himself. He looked Dan in the face. "Daniel, I need to tell you something. Despite the fact that Evelyn's gone now, I think you ought to know what I was going to tell you earlier."

Alex's face was the visual equivalent of the word *solemn*.

"Well, go ahead, then, Alex," Dan said good-naturedly, uncomfortable with Alex's seriousness and trying to put his friend at ease. "It can't make any difference now."

"I hope not," Alex said cryptically.

Dan didn't understand. If the thing with Evelyn was over, how could anything Alex told him be cause for getting upset?

Alex shrugged, then looked steadily at Dan. "Daniel, you ought to know that Evelyn...." He hesitated. "Dan, Evelyn and I...." He stopped again. Then out of the blue, he asked, "Dan, how many law students live on our street in Winston-Salem?"

"Three," Dan replied, gesturing to show his confusion. "You, me, and Honeywell."

"Yes." Alex nodded, then said, measuring his words, "Well, Daniel, all of the law students on our street have slept with Evelyn."

"Oh."

Dan wasn't sure what he thought Alex's revelation might be, but he was sure now that it wasn't that.

"Oh." He sat for a couple of minutes staring at his sandwich.

Alex touched him on the arm. When he looked up, his friend's face was full of genuine concern.

"I... I've always meant to tell you, Dan," he said quietly. "It happened late last summer–while I was visiting Honeywell–around the time that we rented our house. We were together only the one night." He stopped and took a long gulp of tea.

"At the party before Christmas break, when you were with her, I assumed you knew about her. She's sort of... sort of thrown herself at law students all fall. I really can't say if it's marrying a lawyer or just sex that motivates her. I guess–" He stopped suddenly. The alteration in Dan's expression was probably the reason.

"You knew this and let me invite her here?" Dan's eyes were cold blue flames.

"Dan, I'm sorry. I tried to tell you."

"Well, Alex. Is confession good for the soul? Do you feel better *now*?" Dan asked icily.

Alex started to reply, but at that moment Ramona returned to the table. She gave Alex a kiss on the cheek.

Alex's look at her was one of real tenderness; a look such as he had once given Evelyn.

"Well," Ramona said cheerily, seemingly oblivious to the tension, "eat up, gentlemen. I see you've let your sandwiches get cold out of politeness."

She took up her fork, had a bite of her salad, and continued. "I've talked to Audrey. We're all going to her place for dinner tonight. Then we're going to a play. She's gotten free tickets for us all. Something very English. What did she call it? A 'Restoration comedy,' she said. By someone named Congrave, I think. She said you'd know all about it, Dan."

"Congreve," Dan corrected coldly, automatically. "*The Way of the World*, I suppose."

"That's it," she said happily, then took another bite of salad.

Alex and Dan sat in silence.

For the first time she noticed something not right at the table. "So," she said, taking a sip of tea and swallowing carefully, "what have you two been talking about?"

Dan smiled, rather cruelly. It was a moment to test the mettle of a gentleman.

Alex's face turned ashen. He thought for a moment that Dan might tell Ramona about his relations with Evelyn right there at the table.

Dan looked at them both, Alex fearful, Ramona concerned. Something possessed him to say insinuatingly, "We were talking about *how much* we have in common."

"Oh," Ramona said. Confused, she went back to her salad.

Alex's face relaxed visibly.

Dan smiled at him cheerfully, goadingly.

Suddenly, Alex realized that Dan wasn't necessarily talking about Evelyn. His face went stern. He looked at Ramona, then at Dan, then at Ramona again. If Dan meant the suggestion concerning Ramona in jest (which he thought must be the case) his taste was atrocious. If he meant it seriously, Alex simply could not believe it.

Dan said no more. He did not want to be accused of not being a Southern gentleman.

The future lay before them, uncertain and troubling.

The End

About The Author

Jim Booth is a native Southerner, born and bred in North Carolina of Virginia emigrants. He attended college in North Carolina and in New York, where he studied writing. His short fiction has been published both in print and on-line. He currently serves as Director of the Effective Writing Program at the University of Maryland University College. *The New Southern Gentleman* is his first novel.

Jim, Goat Boy